GHOULISH BOOKS
San Antonio Texas
www.GhoulishTales.com

Ghoulish Tales—Issue #3
Copyright © Ghoulish Books 2024
(Individual stories copyright by their respective authors)
All Rights Reserved

ISBN: 978-1-963801-05-7

PUBLISHERS:
Max Booth III & Lori Michelle Booth
EDITOR GHOUL: Max Booth III
LAYOUT DESIGN GHOUL: Lori Michelle Booth
ART GHOUL: Betty Rocksteady
SLUSH ASSISTANT GHOUL: Mindy Rose

CONNECT WITH US

Patreon:
www.patreon.com/ghoulishbooks

Website:
www.Ghoulish.rip

Facebook:
www.facebook.com/GhoulishMagazine

Twitter:
@GhoulishTales

Instagram:
@GhoulishBookstore

Newsletter:
www.PMMPNews.com

Linktree:
www.linktr.ee/ghoulishbooks

THANK YOU TO ALL OUR MEMBERS

Millie Abecassis, Christina Alvarez, Abby Barre, Chris Baumgartner, Ryan Bradley, Bridget Brave, Paul Buchholz, Zachary Chapman, Brandon Choy, Sarah Duck-Mayr, Kenny Endlich, Tony Evans, Jonathan Gensler, Brooke Gessner, Michael Gonzalez, Mason Hawthorne, Matthew Henshaw, Paige Holland, Brian King, Justin Lewis, Rex Long, Anne M Marble, Gregory Martin, Henry Moray, Kristina Osborn, Leane Parsons, Bob Pastorella, Steve Pattee, Helen Patterson, Cynthia Petersen, Christina Pfeiffer, Nicolas Rebena, Daniel Robichaud, Heather Russell, Brad Sanders, Morgan Shine, Jay Slayton-Joslin, Kevin Thomas, Jenny Underwood, Dave Urban, Roger Venable, and Mark Wensel

A SPECIAL THANK YOU TO OUR PATREON SUPPORTERS

A. H. Plotts, Adam Rains, Adrian Shotbolt, Alex Jimanez, Amanda Niehaus-Hard, Antony Klancar, Betty Rocksteady, Bob , Brad Sanders, Bryan, Chazzaroo, Chris Baumgartner, Claudia J Parker, Clay Waters, Cullen Wade, Daniel Scamell, Dave, David Demchuk, David Perlmutter, Emma Williamson, Erin Murphy-Jay, Eve Harms, Fox Morphis, gengar, George Daniel Lea, Grant Longstaff, Heather O'Donnell, Ian Muller, Jack Smiles, James (Tony) Evans, Jampersand, Jason Kawa, Jennifer McCarthy, Jesse Rohrer, Jessica Compean, Jessica McHugh, Joe Z, John Foster, Jose Triana, Joseph Daniels, Julie Cyburt, Kevin Lovecraft, Lisa, Lori Barr, Matthew Booth, Matthew Brandenburg, Matthew Henshaw, miguel_myers_atx, Mistina Picciano, Myrmidon, Nat Weaver, Night Worms, Nikolas P. Robinson, Rebecca , Rob Gibbs, Roger Venable, Ryan Jenkins, Sammynona , Samuel Peirce, Scott Adlerberg, Scotty Nerdrage, Shannon, Shelby MacLeod, Sheri White, Steve Ringman, Stewie, This Is Horror, Thomas Joyce, Todd Keisling, Webberly Rattenkraft, Will Griskevich, and William Hull

DID YOU KNOW GHOULISH BOOKS HAS A PHYSICAL RETAIL STORE?

The rumors are true! We have officially opened our own horror-themed bookstore in the Greater San Antonio Area. In addition to books, we also host weekly movie nights, fun events, and much more!

Come on down to Ghoulish Books at
9330 Corporate Drive, Suite #702,
Selma, TX 78154
for all your spooky needs.

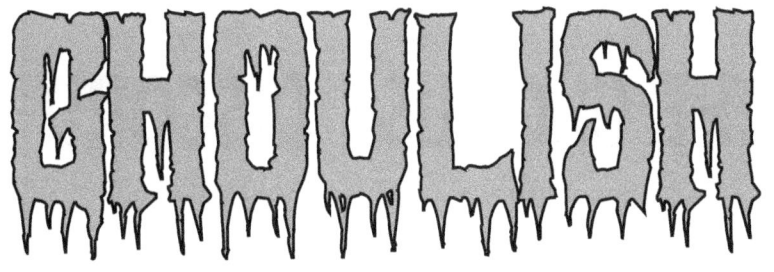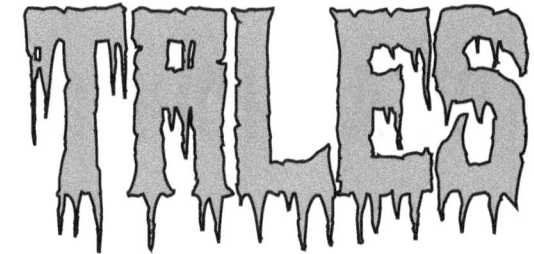

Issue #3

Fiction

Non-Fiction

GHOULISH FOREVER

EVERY ISSUE OF this magazine is a small miracle. Those following along at home might remember this issue originally being advertised as a summer release. We weren't quite able to hit that deadline, and we had to regroup to make this thing an autumn issue. It's hard to describe, exactly, why this was so delayed. I guess it boils down to this being a very small operation with an extremely limited staff that's eager to overcommit themselves to too many projects. Sometimes, to avoid drowning, things have to be pushed. We are extremely grateful to all of the authors involved for their patience.

This is only the third issue of *Ghoulish Tales* but I feel it deep in my bones that this publication is important to the genre. Every story in here absolutely blew me away. When I'm reading slush, I'm actively searching for reasons to reject. We pay 10c per word—so, for example, the issue you hold in your hands cost us just under $3,000. For a small company like ours, that's a huge dent in our bank account. A story must be *incredible* to win us over and convince us to buy it. Especially when you consider none of us are actually profiting from any of this. If we somehow make back the $3k spent on stories, any additional royalties will be recycled into paying for the next issue.

I'm not bringing any of this up to whine, or whatever. I love putting together this magazine. It's one of the coolest things in the world. The only reason we'd even do something like this is because we're deeply passionate and insane. I just want to emphasize the reality of how much time and effort goes into getting something like this off the ground. There are so many moving pieces involved and everything is under constant threat of total burnout. I've lost track of how many times I've internally screamed at myself to work on this magazine and instead opted to stare at the wall without a single thought in my dumb brain. Not because I disliked the quality of the magazine. Not at all. Then why? Harder question to answer. I guess I'm just very tired all of the time. You ever watch that *I Think You Should Leave* sketch with the guy in the shopping mall slumping over and going, *"There's too much fucking shit on me."*? I don't think humans were designed to take on the kind of work some of us do. Certainly not the quantity. It's absurd and silly.

And yet we do it, over and over, with no sign of stopping. To stop is to die, and I want this magazine to live a long, glorious life. I want *Ghoulish Tales* to span decades, not just a couple of years. I want it to be *the* horror fiction magazine. I think it can be. I truly do. Especially with stories like the ones you're about to read. Because holy shit. These stories? These stories are about to rock your world, my spooky friend.

So sit back, and relax, and prepare to discover some of your favorite new authors.

—Max Booth III

Subscribe to
THE GHOULISH TIMES

Keep yourself updated with everything going on in the world of GHOULISH by subscribing to our newsletter, The Ghoulish Times!

Essays, interviews, and even occasional fiction! Plus, photos of our cute dogs.

Everybody in your neighborhood is already subscribed.

WHY AREN'T YOU?

https://buttondown.email/ghoulish

CUTTING A MERMAID IN HALF: THE MAGICIAN'S SECRET REVEALED

Joe Koch

BEFORE THE GUTS splash out and the screaming starts, before Elousa and the girls get wind of what he's done, Jahn imagines running away to the ocean.

This time, it will be mythical, nothing like when he first learned of a world outside aquaculture tanks. He won't end up in a bathtub with a rusted faucet, one senile stream dribbling, blinds drawn dark in the back of a dusty trailer park. He won't have to tell some man everything he wants to hear after doing everything he wants to do to escape ending up as sushi or snuffed on dry land.

"It's a clear shot down the Mississippi," he pleads.

Elousa shifts her abundant black locks over her shoulder and curls around a floating tray of snails, kelp, confections, and champagne. She takes her time pouting and pondering, puckering her lips in elaborate indecision. "You do realize we have it good here. You can't get champagne in the ocean, not without a shipwreck." She continues swirling, turning her back to the customers at the glass and swaying her voluminous shining rump. "Maybe not even then. Not worth risking getting chopped in half by some lunatic."

"I hate champagne. It's a trick, anyway."

They've all heard the whispers. There's a magician looking for a mermaid, but Jahn's buzzed his hair off and starved his chest flat. His hip bones strike out above his scales like coral formations instead of succulent sea-flesh. No one believes a mermaid can be a boy, but Jahn holds his tail straight while others undulate.

"Look," he insists. "It's totally safe. They make a split-compartment box with a fake tailfin that moves by remote control. I researched it. You just ball up in one side before the blade comes down."

Tapping the enclosure, a patron holds up a voucher and three fingers. Jahn rolls his eyes.

Elousa laughs. "Be nice. They'll cum faster." She relishes disciplined sex without giving in to the wild siren's habit of murder, prides her fry on their perfect track record: no accidental deaths. "Seriously, what would we do in the ocean? Hunt?"

Her trailing fingers brush by, lingering long enough to send an electric charge up Jahn's side as she passes him over and gathers two others. He can't deny her love, or any of the girls he's grown up with. He wishes he felt at ease among their circle of sensuous games and ministrations, but something deep in his body rebels.

The cavern below his belly aches with unpleasant hunger and aches much worse when it's filled. The long muscles down to Jahn's tailfin stiffen as he imagines his core engorged, the hunger reversed, and a sea creature expansive enough to plunder. His tail curls forward, upward, rising desirously. A smirk slips onto his face.

And then a man steps out of another century from the shadows, wearing a black velvet cape and top-hat. The head of his cane seems to shift around his fingers like a living tongue, or a tangle of dense tentacles.

Jahn's smirk freezes into a sneer. The man tips his hat.

For three more days he comes, never pressing a ticket to the glass, only emerging when others disperse and the girls leave Jahn alone with the man's black or blue or green-deep shifting eyes, eyes like the color of the sea that Jahn's seen in paintings of shipwrecks, where the sky meets the waves with passionate fury, and the surf foams in rabid tongues that lick at splintering wood and seamen's taut flesh.

The man lingers without demand, and on the fifth day removes his top-hat, pulls out five vouchers, presses them against the glass, and rips them up. He tosses the scraps high and thrusts his hat upside-down to catch them.

They vanish.

The man shrugs. He turns to depart, but when he flips his hat over his head, five vouchers flutter down about his shoulders intact. He catches one in his mouth. Jahn laughs.

The man's tongue whips out. His expression is deadly. His eyes seize and strangle Jahn's gaze and he chews the voucher voraciously, frothingly, and then swallows it with a deep writhing gulp and opens wide to show an empty maw. His breath fogs the glass between them.

Jahn dismisses his rage at being carried, splashes down the enclosure's exit ramp, and absconds wrapped in the magician's cape. He doesn't stop to say farewell to the girls.

In private, the magician hands Jahn his cane. It moves strangely, like an eel. Jahn licks it as the magician strips. It tastes of salt. The man gasps as though caressed.

He goes down on all fours and Jahn spreads him, slick lubricious fish skin sliding upon the man's back, scales grinding his ass. Jahn's tail curls between the magician's legs and slaps at his prick. The cane slithers away as he plunges fingers in the magician and bites his neck, lost in the rocking motion of the sea between them. Something prods Jahn's shark-like slit, his hardening hunger, and before he can act, the moist parasite penetrates and clamps. Nerve endings and blood flow connect, and Jahn feels the eel's sensations as his own.

The tip of the eel bolts into the pucker where Jahn's fingers have softened the magician. Swallowing and swallowed, Jahn clenches the man's cock in his thick curling tail, completing the circle of an ouroboros, as if the two of them are one great sea-monster, the descending heart of the maelstrom, the rising eye of a murderous typhoon.

Rehearsals go well. Tickets sell out. Repeat performances draw bigger crowds each week. The magician hints at a coastal tour. Jahn grows his hair out for the show. The trick is perfectly safe.

Contentment brings a hint of Jahn's curves, and more surface with growing discontent. Joy in his land-pampered body becomes disgust. The shared eel is not enough. "None of this is mine," he says. "When are we going to the ocean?" He hates the whine abrading his voice, but can't stop crying. "You promised."

The magician pantomimes care, an honest farce, feeding Jahn a sardine and stroking the swell of his scaled hip. He waves a gloved hand. A folded note materializes that says: *I love you as a man, no matter how you think you look.*

The curtains rise. The crowds applaud. No one believes a mermaid can be a boy, but Jahn holds his tail straight while cowards undulate. The trick relies on a specially constructed box, a fake tailfin, and Jahn's limber constriction before the blade drops. It's perfectly safe. Unless Jahn gives up on reaching the ocean, unless hunger reversed grows a deeper pit, unless Jahn chooses the chopping block over the fairy tale.

He imagines death like running away.

This time, he won't trade a trap for another trap.

When his guts splash out and the screaming starts, the magician grabs Jahn's face in agonized passion, moving so fast he slips and flails in the bisected gore of him. The dark smell of exposed innards is a fever between them. There's no ocean, no freedom, no circling back, only the black fire of pain and Jahn's sick satisfied terror at killing a myth.

TOXICITY

MAX BOOTH III

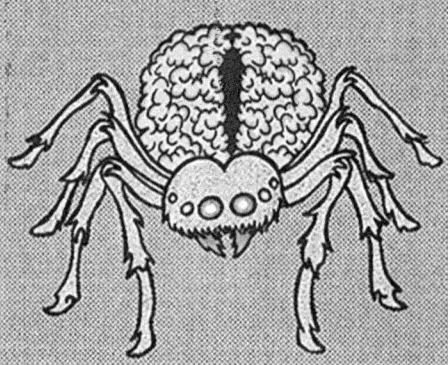

THE MIND IS A RAZORBLADE

MAX BOOTH III

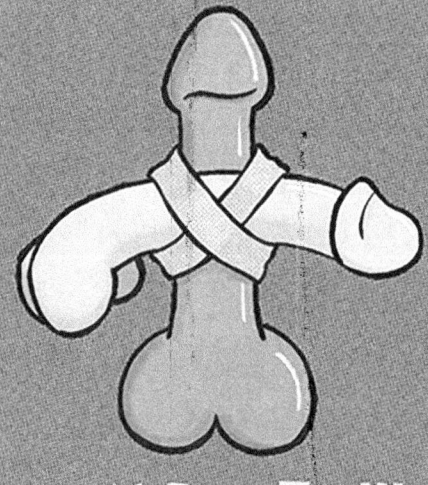

HOW TO SUCCESSFULLY KIDNAP STRANGERS

MAX BOOTH III

WWW.GHOULISH.RIP

RED CARNAGE OR BUST

Xochilt Avila

WHEN DENNIS SAW the announcement, he was half-convinced it was a joke. Drunkenness still lacquered his brain, his temples pulsing from the chlorine stench that clung to his freckled skin. But the website confirmed it.

It was official.

That upcoming Friday marked the last day theme park enthusiasts could pilgrimage to Westminster, Maryland to experience Thrillzone's infamous roller coaster, Red Carnage. This meant Dennis Miller, and his coaster aficionado twin brother Jimmy, needed to hustle.

The ginger boy paced across the fraying dining room rug, his waterlogged Vans squelching beneath his feet. They were too-tight remnants of middle school, now pinching at his toes. Occasionally Dennis peeked into the living room as though to find something new, something other than open liquor bottles and pizza crusts littered across the table. And, of course, the limp form on the couch, still just as sopping wet as he was.

They only had *four days*. Four days to cross several state lines and reach Thrillzone in time to make Jimmy's dream a reality.

Though Dennis had always felt lukewarm about Red Carnage, he knew Jimmy thought about the old-school coaster nonstop. There wasn't anything his brother cared about more than the speeding, rumbling, *stomach-in-your-ass-dropping* world of roller coasters.

It was a love that stemmed from the state fairs of their childhood, when the twins had finally sprouted tall enough to ride a rickety old contraption, its carts molded into hideous dragons that soared at a grand speed of ten miles per hour. The ride had barely left an impression on Dennis, but Jimmy would chatter about it all day, begging to go on again and again, until it drove their parents nutty. When he wasn't riding coasters, he talked about them, usually with Dennis (given that neither had many friends).

In a life plagued with high school bullying and apathetic officials who bemoaned the chore of maintaining 504s, roller coasters provided true happiness for Jimmy, and Dennis couldn't help but share in his brother's joy. In coasters, they could escape the monotony of Midwest corn fields and a failing public education system.

Since turning fifteen, the duo had graduated from mowing neighbors' lawns to flipping Culver's burgers after school and during breaks, allowing the blue-collared boys to visit nearly every Wyoming park. But this summer was supposed to be when they scratched Red Carnage off their bucket list. In a month, they could have snagged a used car off Marketplace. By September, they could have booked the hotel. Dennis had wanted to go just before the start of senior year, to have something warm and precious for Jimmy to hold onto.

Now their plan would most certainly need adjustments.

Obviously, because Red Carnage was closing in less than a week. But, more importantly, because Jimmy Miller had drowned and died in their pool an hour before Dennis had even *seen* Thrillzone's announcement. Arguably, that was an even worse complication. But as the young boy gazed upon the body of his twin, he resolved himself to what had to be done, scrambling to collect road snacks and their parents' car keys. This wouldn't deter him. He wouldn't let anything stop him from making his brother's dream come true.

***

Damp amber curls clung to Dennis' forehead as he barreled down the interstate, still a hair tipsy from their liquor cabinet excursion. Now elbow-deep in Nebraska, 4:25 AM flashed in the corner of his heavy eye. The AC's arctic blast kept him alert, as did his sharp awareness of the revolver tucked away in the glove compartment.

Their father had taught Dennis how to shoot last Christmas break, allowing him to fire once or twice to scare off the mountain lions. Jimmy hadn't even bothered to hold the gun, let alone use it. Back then Dennis had cackled when his brother squirmed and sobbed at the sudden, trembling boom. It wasn't particularly funny anymore. He sighed and turned the dial until he found something other than static.

"Good thing Ma and Pa decided to fly to the wedding," Dennis broke the silence, refocusing his attention on the long stretch of asphalt ahead. "They'll be mad we took the car, of course, but at least I got my license. Unlike you."

Of course, there wasn't a reply. There wouldn't be one. Dennis understood what was happening. He wasn't delusional. But it was a *long* road from Wyoming to Maryland, and just because Jimmy had lungs full of water didn't mean he deserved to be *bored* the whole way. But try as he did, Jimmy wasn't a particularly good conversationalist, at least when it didn't concern his interests. Soon enough Dennis stopped talking, his mind wandering once again.

Though they lived halfway across the country, Jimmy adored Red Carnage more than his brother had ever understood. Upon first glance, the crimson attraction appeared modest at best and laughably obsolete at worst. Most parkgoers considered it Thrillzone's worst attraction. It neither towered as high as Doctor Danger's Doomsday Drop nor whistled and danced like the buckaroo skeletons that beckoned riders to brave Big Billy's Bone Rattler.

Red Carnage was simpler, Jimmy had always insisted to his brother. Better. *Finessed.* Red Carnage didn't need bread and circuses, as their ma would say.

The mechanical beast, a robust steel coaster designed by a now-defunct manufacturer, cycled through nine inversions during its sporadic run before ending with a terrifying descend and body-slamming roll. Devilish animatronics taunted riders as they were pulled along, giggling and spewing flames from their cackling grins. All of this while reaching speeds of up to seventy miles per hour and all while making its riders deeply, painfully uncomfortable.

Even in the early days, before the newer and flashier rides, Red Carnage had been labeled a rattling, disjointed mess. For every fan of the tumultuous attraction, there were at least a dozen who flooded theme park forums to bemoan the ride's janky turns and neck-spraining drops.

But Jimmy would explain that that was the *point* of Red Carnage. Discomfort was an artistic intention, sewn into the fabric of the ride's DNA.

Like many attractions, Red Carnage followed a loose narrative. A massive demonic head welcomed adventurers into a gaping maw, its esophagus leading them toward withered, rust-colored ferry boats. The sudden stomach-dropping force would rip riders away from their mortal coils, descending them across every circle of hell.

Jimmy's deep web sleuths had given the brothers insight into the miserable life of the ride's head designer, Isai Egorov. Xeroxed news clippings and historical archives painted the image of a determined, talented, and deeply miserable man. A nihilistic engineer who had immigrated fresh from the emotional trauma of the Soviet breakdown, who rang out every drop of his soul across a decade of his life to reach Red Carnage's completion. Even if it would end his life in the end.

The boys had once stumbled across Reddit user SteamyHam-722, who claimed to have an uncle who'd worked alongside Egorov in the late nineties. Allegedly, the overworked engineers were to run one last test of the coaster before arranging shipment. Near delirious from time crunch, Egorov pushed against protocol to ride the coaster himself, refusing to leave his cart until someone pressed start. All had seemed well until, at the peak of nearly eighty feet, the engineer supposedly snapped his seatbelt and launched himself down to splat across the factory floor. Desperate to maintain the sale, the manufacturer had kept the suicide under wraps, going so far as to bribe the uncle and his colleagues to smuggle the body into the ravine it was eventually found in.

Dennis didn't know if he believed all *that*, but the tale had utterly transfixed Jimmy. Ultimately, the urban legend added to the attraction's mystique, making it far more than your typical cookie-cutter theme park ride. It was a once-in-a-lifetime experience, one that the pair had coveted for years. And now, they had found themselves here. Dennis scrounged around in the darkness until he found an unopened can of orange pop.

"Guess you were bankin' I'd drive you around so you didn't have to learn, huh?" The exhausted teen scrunched his nose as he sipped. "Guess you were right. Hm. Wonder if I should have told Grace I was leaving. Bet her parents'll be happy. You know they never liked me. Assholes."

Yeah, I mean, nobody wants ugly grandkids, Denny.

Of course, Jimmy didn't *really* speak, but it's precisely what he *would've* said, and that was enough to coax a mirthful laugh from his sleep-deprived brother. "Man, fuck you!"

Cheese puffs flew into the back of the van, a stray few catching in the cadaver's ginger mop. Jimmy's clothes were still soaked, hanging heavy over his pale, spindly frame. His eyes, milky and wide in the rearview mirror, gazed back at Dennis and nothing at all.

"We're gonna make it, Jimmy," Dennis promised, the whisper of dawn beginning to kiss the edge of the world. He peeked at it through a film of fresh tears. "Red Carnage, *or bust*."

***

It was a tragedy that the brothers were so short on time. They'd always wanted to savor this journey, from the open skies and sprawling green hills to the greasy roadside diners and gas station confections. Dennis had even hoped to sneak into one of the adult stores lining the highways between the "Hell is Real" and "Grandpa's Cheese Barn" billboards.

You could go if you wanted, Denny. It's not like I'm going anywhere.

Dennis shook his head, keeping his eyes on the endless road. He knew it would break Jimmy's heart to miss the chance to laugh at some roadside dildos or swipe a nudie mag. He just couldn't do it. It wasn't fun if it wasn't the two of them together.

"We stick together, man. And we really don't have the time for it anyway."

Yeah, guess it's already Wednesday.

"That and we're in the middle of summer. This AC isn't gonna last forever, and you're starting to get funky."

Dennis could almost hear the snort of indignance. *No worse than your room, Denny,* his brother would say through wheezing laughter. The young ginger tried to imagine it, and tried to ignore the flitting fear that he'd someday forget how his brother's laughter sounded.

Unfortunately, though, Wednesday brought fresh light to Dennis' fears. About a half hour out of Columbus, the AC wheezed its last miserable breath. *"Fuck,"* the boy hissed, slamming his fists on the useless vents. He didn't expect it to help, and it absolutely didn't.

The July heat creeped inward, baking the steel van with a pungent and fruity decay. The older twin managed to uncover an old, sticky bottle of Scentsy from underneath his seat, but spraying every ounce barely put a dent in the wretched stink. Now the van was ripe with decomposition *and* Sassy Pineapples.

At least he'd had the sense to block out the backseat windows with cardboard the night before. Nobody could see Jimmy, his face now heavy with bloat and discolorment, his lips full and nose seeping with bloody foam. But it wouldn't do them much good if someone managed to *smell* him.

Dennis ground his teeth and battled nausea for four more miles before the stench forced him to pull over and throw open the driver's door. The dirt below was drenched in putrid orange and nibbles of Slim Jims as he hurled and prayed nobody passing paid too close attention. Back and forth, Dennis weighed his odds, but eventually, he conceded and cracked the driver-side window as he continued onward.

Blessedly, the night brought coolness, which marginally quelled the simmering rot. But by then Dennis had begun to skirt the edge of consciousness, anyway. The van swayed back and forth as they passed the welcome sign for Pennsylvania. Dennis prayed that the cops wouldn't notice. Quietly, he asked Jimmy to pray with him.

***

"Will that be all?"

" . . . Sorry?"

The teen blinked his weariness away, his brain chugging to process what his ears had supposedly heard. Dazed eyes studied the swollen bags of cheesy chips and sugary energy drinks. Food. Right. A lethargic hand fished inside his hoodie until it excavated a crumpled twenty. "Can I put the change on number five . . . ?"

Dennis dropped the bill on the counter as he glanced back out the window. A sun-degraded car touting a Penn State grad on the bumper had pulled into the lot, settling a couple of rows away from the van. Outside, a gray-haired man stood at the pump, his square face contorted in a grimace. Dennis watched him mouth to his wife in the passenger seat.

What's that smell?

Gut punches ricocheted across the grease-soaked walls of Dennis' stomach, jolting his mind to full attention. He looked back to the cashier, who'd already completed the transaction, her eyes narrowed in scrutinization as she held his receipt. The eyes of suspicion. The eyes of someone seconds away from asking *if he was alright,* and who knew how long away from calling the cops. Suddenly, Dennis was cognizant of how he looked, of the foul bouquet that clung to his wrinkled clothes and unwashed hair.

But they needed the gas. They wouldn't make it otherwise.

The longest stretch of the young boy's life ticked on before the underpaid clerk finally spoke again, tone thick with caution. " . . . Your receipt." The slip was placed on the counter and distinctly *not* in Dennis' clammy fingers. He snatched it up along with his snacks, his calm facade shattering as soon as he stepped outside. Somehow, God had favored the wayward boy enough to urge the old Toyota along its way, leaving him alone in the lot with Jimmy in the SUV.

Dennis' fingers felt damp around the nozzle as he filled the tank. Even with inches of metal between them, his brother's sugary rot punched through his nostrils, squeezing its grip around his stomach. His decision to keep the window cracked had beckoned a small army of flies, their little bodies wriggling between the layers of glass and cardboard for all to see. The old man from before had no business driving if he hadn't seen all the squirming, buzzing dots. *Another stroke of luck*, Dennis mused, feeling like the least lucky person in Pennsylvania as he screwed on the cap.

Reluctantly, he forced himself back inside the rancid vehicle. Mere hours separated them from their destination. It was a finish line that rekindled the exhausted boy's determination and willed his foot on the gas. Dennis smiled at the bloated boy behind him as they pulled out from the lot. One last glance toward the store showed the cashier at the window, her eyes following the vehicle all the way until it pulled onto the interstate.

***

The boys were in Maryland. Finally. After the longest road trip of their young lives, Dennis and Jimmy Miller had made it to the crab state. And they were so very, very close to their destination. Since they passed the border, they'd been bombarded with the park's billboards. Now, hours later, Dennis could *see* the exit up ahead, advertising all young and old to embrace the heart-stopping fun to be had at Thrillzone. Tears trickled down Dennis' grin as he weaved through cars and diesel trucks, undeterred by anything that might try and stop him.

Such as the half-dozen police cars pulsing red and blue behind him, their sirens long since deaf on his ears. All he could hear was the rattling of coaster wheels on steel tracks ahead.

"We're going to make it, Jimmy," Dennis promised, pawing at the wetness on his shallowed cheeks. "We're really going to make it!"

News choppers had joined the hectic pursuit of the SUV, but Dennis remained unwavering. With a sudden right jerk of the wheel, they were off the highway. The streets leading to the park were packed, but Dennis made do with skirting the sidewalk. Pedestrians screamed and skirmished atop one another to escape. Dennis ignored their shrieks, ignored their fear, ignored the frail old woman who bounced off his hood. His attention was zeroed in on the corpse in the backseat and the rapidly approaching gates.

"We did it! Can you believe it?! We're in Thrillzone!! Isn't this so cool??"

You can still turn around, Denny. You can stop this. They'll forgive you.

Dennis whipped his head *no* as the van blasted through the welcome arch and into the parking lot. They flew past terrified couples sporting matching shirts, past soccer moms thrusting baby strollers away with Herculean strength.

"It's too late, Jimmy."

It isn't. They'll forgive you.

The SUV crashed through the electronic turnstiles, flinging metal chunks into souvenir stalls and unfortunate tourists. Blue veins thick like juicy worms throbbed in Dennis' pale neck. His heartbeat drummed out the outer world from his ears. So close. *They were so close.*

"They won't forgive me, Jimmy. Nobody's gonna. Don't you get it? I fucked up. I should have been keeping an eye on you. I'm the older one. I'm the one who looks out for you."

I forgive you, Jimmy.

"YOU SHOULDN'T! IT WAS MY FAULT!"

They sped past churro stands, gunslinging skeletons, and panicked guests in the queue for Doctor Danger. Everyone hurried into a frenzy, with no time to consider where their bodies needed to move to avoid the danger. Later reports would cite dozens of deaths due to this particular stampede.

It was an accident. We were drinking. You didn't see me get in the water.

"That's not an excuse. *That's not a fucking excuse.* But I'm making it up to you!"

Finally, the massive crimson coaster came into view, its glowing sign crowning the top of a massive, grinning devil's head. Red Carnage. The journey was over.

Dennis braked, the massive car's tires squealing atop concrete never meant for such traction. He stopped shy of ramming into the ride's waiting patrons, who eagerly disintegrated into the shrieking mobs.

Gasping, Dennis opened the door, releasing a cloud of fat flies as he stumbled into chaos on his jellied legs. He only heard the sirens distantly, which meant the cops hadn't dared mimic his reckless driving. It gave them a sliver of time, but not much more than that. He had to think quickly.

Amongst the flurry of bodies, Dennis found what he needed: an employee hiding behind a nearby podium, donned in khaki shorts and the park's trademark *Thrilling Teal* polo. Bernard, his nametag read, from York, Pennsylvania. He didn't look much older than Dennis, but by the looks of the biceps spilling out of his uniform, he was definitely stronger.

"YOU! Can you operate Carnage?"

"Uhh?" Bernard stammered, cautiously coming into view. "I . . . uh . . . Fuck. Yeah??"

From inside his hoodie, the manic teen unveiled his father's pistol. "You're gonna help me get my brother on it, and then you're gonna turn it the fuck on."

"Oh god, okay, fuck! Sure! Just don't fucking shoot me?" Like a fresh fawn still slick with birth, Bernard scrambled toward the van, only to stop as he saw what awaited behind the door. Amidst the mayhem, the cardboard had slipped off from the windows, unveiling a crawling biome of humming blowflies and maggots wriggling across the grimed glass. Revulsion anchored the park employee's no-slip shoes until Dennis blasted a warning shot into the air.

"Now."

"Okay, okay, okay!" Benard slowly opened the backseat with a loud, wet gag. "Oh god, *oh fuck,* I should have been a lifeguard—"

"Be careful with him." Dennis looked up to the helicopters. Heart ramming against his ribs, he turned toward the coaster's entrance, staring down the demon head's enticing grin. "Pick him up and follow me."

More terrified than repulsed, the employee did as instructed, hands trembling as they unbuckled the cadaver's seatbelt. Jimmy's collapsing form sat bloated and bruised, purple skin sloughing and damp from dissolving enzymes. The body's release from the upholstery bloomed yet another waft of rotten fumes, now seemingly from the dark ichor that seeped down the dead boy's jeans.

"Oh god. I can't do it—"

"Do it, or I'm going to shoot you. *I'm not joking.*"

Bernard wept, still gagging as he fully pulled out the corpse. Jimmy's body sagged as though melting in the young boy's arms, but he was held steady enough. Dennis nodded, satisfied, and gestured with his gun for the employee to move through the devil's grin.

"Express lane. Let's go."

Dennis followed Bernard down the shortened pathway built for those who shilled out over a grand a year to become Annual Thrill Seekers. Despite the unfolding scene, he couldn't help but smile. It would have been a thousand times better if Jimmy could walk unassisted, but he knew his brother was having a good time. Maybe they'd be able to ride it twice before the cops finally showed up. "Isn't the queue neat, Jimmy?" The inside hallway resembled a massive esophagus, its walls fleshy pink and spritzed by recurring misters to resemble saliva. It dribbled onto the boys as they moved, Dennis bouncing in his steps, Bernard desperate to escape his putrid hostage. Quickly the trio reached the onboarding ramp, with an empty ferry boat already waiting at the start of the ride.

"Put him in." Dennis gestured to the cart, his palms so damp the gun nearly slipped from his grasp. From the entrance, he heard a building commotion: the echo of voices and radios and growling dogs. "Put him in then start the fucking ride!"

Bernard eagerly dumped the corpse into the faux boat's front seat, clearly on the verge of a breakdown. He shook residue off his arms as he scrambled to the control station while Dennis quickly jumped into the seat beside his brother. He sloppily pulled down the safety bar, pistol still in hand, his body pulsing with anticipation.

A voice suddenly bellowed from the ride's intercom, raw and coarse as graveyard gravel. It spoke over the sounds of police rushing to the scene, brandishing their guns and snarling canines. *"Riders . . . are you ready . . . for CARNAGE???"*

"YES! YES!" Dennis shrieked, his free hand snatching his brother's limp wrist to hold their hands in the air.

"Get out of the ride!" an officer ordered as he approached the brothers. "Get out of the ride and put your weapon down!"

"Are you ready . . . to brave what hell awaits?"

"WE DID IT, JIMMY! WE DID IT!"

Dennis, please listen to them.

"Sir, step out of the ride IMMEDIATELY."

"Very well. But don't say you weren't warned—"

Beneath Dennis the cart jostled and hummed, swaying back slightly as mechanisms shifted, readying for launch. He beamed at the nearby police and chucked his gun into the crowd, spurring them to leap away from the ramp. They couldn't stop it. Nothing could stop it.

And then, suddenly, speed.

Speed.

Dennis shrieked as sudden force ripped the ferry boat forward, barreling the brothers into a fleshy inner tunnel. Commands rang behind them, but everything was soon drowned by the jostling steel cart beginning its first incline. The ride's track flipped between the enclosed, flesh-colored tunnels and open-air space as they steadily climbed one of Thrillzone's greatest heights. Through these gaps, Dennis could see his wake of destruction, from smoldering fires along the highway to the flashes of red and blue scattered across the parking lot. He smiled serenely, his fingers lacing with his brother's bloated, sagging hand as they finally reached the first peak.

There, atop the precedence of Red Carnage, Dennis could only see the lush horizon of Northern Maryland. He could only hear the rippling roar of air. He could only feel his brother's hand in his own, and on such a bright summer day, he could almost believe it to be warm. For a precious and meager eternity on top of the world, Dennis was happier than he'd ever been. Happier than he knew he'd ever be again.

And then, slowly, the ferry boat lurked and moved down, down, *down.*

Dennis had anticipated the first inversion, having watched countless POV videos from Jimmy through the years. But still, it hurt no less; The turn still felt too sudden, bumping his body against his brother's corpse and the steel edge of his little cart. As though it was designed to hurt. Jimmy's voice echoed between his brother's wide, glistening eyes:

That's the whole point of Red Carnage.

Turn after turn, the trembling ferry boat scrambled across the steel lines, each jerk flaring yet another burst of agony through Dennis' body. Teeth clamped, he braced himself, his grip so tight on Jimmy's hand he could feel the ripe skin sliding from the muscle. This was *fun*, he was having *fun*, he was having the *time of his life*. He just needed to push through his delirium. That's why he was in so much pain. That's why, despite knowing that

Carnage was an above-ground ride, he continued to descend farther and farther with every wicked twist and turn.

But how long had it been since he'd seen the red and blue lights that colored *Thrillzone*? How long had it been since he'd smelled burning rubber or heard blaring sirens? All he could see were the slick, pink tunnels, alit by pulsing veins that bathed the passage in a sickly crimson. And the impish animatronics, each eager to shoot flames from its grinning muzzle. Each fiery plume inched closer until Dennis had to slap the singe away from his bangs.

"What the fuck is going on?!"

Do you think hell is for the dead?

The tunnel rumbled with the ride's voiceover, so loud that Dennis could feel it vibrate through the crooked teeth in his skull.

Sweet boys. Didn't you know? Hell is for the living.

More fire blasted at the cart from the shadows, bathing the brothers in licks of wicked heat. Dennis shrieked, frantically patting at his hair and clothes. His ears flooded with his own panic, he couldn't hear the faint sounds of another nearby, the miserable, wet gargles passing through puffed, foamy lips. He didn't notice the shifting weight of the rotting mass in the seat beside him. Not until the swollen hand he held onto squeezed back. Dennis froze, unconcerned as to how his reddened skin seared with pain.

Hell is here and now.

"Den . . . ny . . . ?"

Somehow, over the cacophony of screeching metal and cackling puppets, Dennis heard it. A sound croaked through congealed blood and putrid slop backed up from the corpse's collapsing stomach. No, not a sound. *A voice.*

Dennis jerked as far across the cart as he could go, his hand leaving his brother's so quickly he watched the skin flake off the muscle with ease. He shrieked, chuckling the useless flap of flesh into the tunnel. With slow, sickening twitches, the bare fingers curled and released, pushing through the settlement of rigor mortis. Spinal bones cracked as the corpse's head snapped left, the pale, leaking eyes of Jimmy Miller finding his petrified brother.

"*Denny?*"

"Oh god. Oh god."

"*Denny . . . where . . . are . . . we?*"

Sunlight assaulted Jimmy's vision as the tunnel abruptly ended. The duo was back outside, overlooking the massacre spread across Thrillzone as they approached Carnage's finale. Dennis could see his brother's oozing face so much clearer now. His skin was pocked with countless little holes, no longer just from ache, but from where juicy maggots had sprung and feasted. Horrifically mangled and so obviously dead.

"Oh god, oh god, oh FUCKING GOD—" The winds swallowed Dennis' screams, the teen panicked with nowhere to run. Beside him the corpse fidgeted, its rotting hands grasping at the living teen's hoodie. The raw, wet muscles of the exposed hand glowed beneath the sun's rays.

"*Denny . . . Denny, please . . . I'm scared.*"

The ferryboat halted, resting at the attraction's crescendo. A second helicopter had joined the first, so close now that Dennis could hear the whipping blades over the air currents. He gulped for air, eyes uncertain as he sized up his decaying twin. Even through the gore and fluids and revulsion . . . he could see it. Jimmy *was* afraid. And Jimmy was *here*. With *him*. Cautiously, he inched closer.

" . . . It's . . . it's okay, Jimmy. You're with me. We're on Red Carnage."

"*Carnage?*"

"Yeah . . . We made it, Jimmy. Can you believe it?"

"*You . . . did this? For me?*"

Dennis nodded, his smile uncertain. He knew that whatever awaited him beyond these tracks, he deserved it. It would be painful. It would be *hell.* But he wouldn't be a coward, and he wouldn't abandon the one remaining tether to this life. *This* wasn't a punishment, he realized. Carnage wanted them to ride together as much as they'd wanted to ride Carnage.

Shifting cautiously, Dennis again entwined his fingers with his brother's skinless grasp. He beamed at the living corpse, and though it made his stomach lurk, he couldn't help but feel joy when Jimmy's sagging lips grinned back. Together, the brothers rose their arms toward the July skies just as the ferryboat tipped over the final peak's edge. Together, they caved into their joyous shrieks, embracing their final marker of boyhood as they descended into the unknown.

THE THREE DEATHS OF THE BLUE MOON RIPPER

Amanda Cecelia Lang

Number Four—The Bitch with the Butterfly Tattoos

SOMETHING'S DIFFERENT ABOUT Number Four. She smells spooky. I climb inside her broken window, fever in my veins and moonlight on my back, and find her wide-asleep in bed, eyes open but faraway, obsidian pupils collecting moondust.

Instead of bubblegum innocence and pop-star pin-ups, Number Four's midnight bedroom haunts of ancient mud and cobwebs, and something scratches inside the grimy walls. She doesn't flinch as I lean over her in my piggy mask and shackles, doesn't scream like the others as rising consciousness shifts her dusty gaze my way. So damn lovely up close, this mystic creature of silken nightgown and bare shoulders, inked skin and silver piercings.

She accelerates my fever.

I push back against the rising hackles of spine and the splitting of skin, lunar toxins boiling my veins. I brandish the shackles. They won't contain my beast—they'll keep Number Four in place for it. But as I capture her wrists, this one doesn't thrash or beg to deaf gods. She watches me, paralyzed by a tranquil terrible awe, redolent of formaldehyde and grave roses, as if she's a corpse already. And now she smiles.

The unexpected thrill of it shoves me back a step, into the burning full lunar light. Brazen, that smile, eerie and dauntless. My moon-drunk heartbeat rages faster, blood like quickfire, difficult to control. My skin overheats now with sweat and bulge, flesh prickling, blistering, aching to crack open and expose the feral menace inside. But something crunches beneath my bare feet. Slimy papery membranes.

Cocoons?

The fever cools a degree. All around, shadows spasm in the high cobwebs. Squirmy bugs snagged in spider-silk. Are those . . . ? I blink, my moon-lathed vision sharp and disbelieving. More oozing chrysalises encrust the walls like tiny vacant death shrouds. And Number Four's tattoos—they twitch and rise. Inky bruises crawl along her bare shoulders, wormy with spider-bent legs and dusty black wings. Fucking butterflies, I hate butterflies.

The scratching inside the walls grows louder. Number Four's lips ripple and tiny insectile legs poke through like hatchlings.

"Shall we begin?" she hisses inside my skull, and an eerie bile of *déjà vu* sicks up inside me. My words. Words I've spoken three times before. *Shall we begin . . . ?*

Her smile unhinges, and eyes glitter inside her throat, multi-faceted, savage, cursed. They explode from her mouth. A furious fluttering black mist! Chaotic wings swarm my piggy mask and squeeze inside, infesting me. Velvet bodies invade my mouth, wiggle up my nostrils, ears, the hollows of my eyes, filling me, smothering my fever, blacking out my moonlight.

Fucking butterflies!

I thrash and beat at my head, choking on spotted wings, gasping for moonlight, gasping for transformation. Where has the fever gone? I claw at myself, clawing, clawing before the eggflies have their slippery way with me.

I transform, I do, bones cracking. But I can't feel the moonlight.

My deep-throated snarl becomes a trio of screaming voices.

Then darkness beats wing and drags me under.

Number One—The Virgin with the Dandelion Hair

I wake atop someone else's moonlit bed, choking. My voice rasps, hideously effeminate, and something parasitic squirms inside my airpipe, foreign, slick. I curl fetal beneath perfumed bedsheets, hacking it up, birthing it from the parting chrysalis of my lips. A wet spasm of wings.

A butterfly.

Fully formed, it flits a spiral across the room and settles on floral wallpaper. Black wings with pale blue spots like glowing moons.

I glare, refusing to tremble. The fuck is this?

They call me the Blue Moon Ripper. Not because I do my savage-work beneath the full moon— though I do—and not because I rip my girls apart without leaving a trace of myself, no fingerprints, no human DNA. But because something *does* remain. Every time. The first, I barely noticed. The second, I dismissed the coincidence. But the third time, detectives christened me a serial killer and named me after the Blue Moon butterflies found in every victim's bedroom. They think the butterflies are my calling card.

But they're not mine.

Half-groggy and cool of vein, I stagger off the ruffled mattress, move barefoot across the plush fuchsia carpet. The butterfly sticks to the wall, just above a perfume-bottle vanity, wings pulsing a slow heartbeat. I tighten a fist, eager to pound the wretched eggfly into a velvet paste. Except my limbs feel noodle-weak and languid, and this bedroom's teen-bop posters and bubblegum frill are distracting and familiar. I glimpse a dewy face in the vanity's mirror and freeze like the predator I am. Amber freckles, golden halo-puff of dandelion hair, willowy and supple for the plucking.

My muscles tense and stiffen, hunter scenting prey.

I know this girl. Not her name, but her number—Number One. This is her bedroom, her lair of pink lip-gloss and stuffed animals and wistful teen romance novels. Last time I was here, everything was dripping, and this one was home alone for the weekend. Wrists so thin, they nearly slipped the shackles.

Soft-footing the doe, I shadow closer—and so does my girl in the mirror.

"Relax, sweetheart, I'm just passing by," I say, but the mirror-girl mouths the words, and my voice isn't mine. I touch my throat and my smooth, beardless chin. So does my reflection. An obscene thrill prickles through me—because I'm *wearing* this girl, a wolf possessing maiden flesh. "The hell?"

Somewhere in the house, glass breaks.

Footsteps haunt the hallway, floorboards moaning outside the bedroom door.

Instantly—fascinating how fast it happens—a musky dire terror pumps through this body I wear, the primal pulse-beat of woodland prey and hunted girls. Moonlight blazes through the window, radiant and dominant and overbright, offering up no shadows to hide in.

No time to close the curtains. The bedroom door moans inward, and a man steps inside. Naked and breathing hard, fevered muscles twitching, shoulders bulging, gloriously obscene, he wears only a greasy rubber piggy mask. Yellow-eyed beneath. Can that be me? It's like having double vision, hyper-real yet eerily transcendent.

I stand in awe of myself. And I remember this moment. How surprised I was to find the girl with the dandelion hair already awake and posing in front of her vanity. Her mangled gasp of terror— the sound that now escapes me.

Reality becomes a mirror, dizzy and inverse, existentially backwards. Fear tastes like dusty wings in my mouth.

The man in the piggy mask produces a set of shackles. He locks one cuff around himself, then tosses me the open end. A familiar metallic clatter. I catch it in delicate waifish hands and perform for myself an eerie, obedient favor. Hands trembling against this body's adrenaline instincts, I snap the cuff around my pale freckled wrist, like a perverse umbilical cord, merging two souls together.

The man in the piggy mask steps into the moonlight, closing in, dwarfing me.

"Shall we begin?"

I've never watched myself transform before. Only felt the exquisite agony from the inside out, the crackling and straining of bones against the skin, the peeling away of tendons and flesh, the savage whetting of fangs.

This outsider perspective is a gift. To wear virgin eyes, to witness my own divinity.

Then the beast before me snarls, scenting the vulnerable freckled flesh I wear.

Gruesome terror eclipses my awe, black-winged and swift as death, another involuntary blood-rush of mortal panic. Our conjoined chains tremble, and the monster he's become lunges. A beast of rabid, gleeful hunger, of flesh-stained misshapen nightmares.

Our rapture should be transcendent, but there's nothing exquisite about this agony.

Number Two—The Slut with the Swollen Eyes

When I wake this second time, I come up ravaged. Invasive fangs and saliva still sinking through me, still defiling me, still cutting soul-deep scars even as I wear new flesh. I clutch at my throat, gagging on silent screams that transform into wings.

A butterfly squirms free of me, slick and unfurling.

Its oily silhouette teases the oily dark. These new eyes I wear come crusty and sore, and I can still feel the foggy weight of tears inside my lungs. The room has changed. Still not my own, though still familiar. Brown, austere, check-out times on the door, black-out drapes, probably a Bible in the drawer, for all the good it's worth. A table-lamp casts sallow light over a nightstand and two fallen bottles. One of pills and one of booze. This one—this pathetic wasted body I now wear—wept and sniveled and self-loathed herself into a blackout sleep.

Don't know *what* woke me.

Maybe the beast standing at the foot of the bed.

I can just make out the outline of the man's piggy mask—of *my* mask—and the intimate naked cut of flank and shoulder. I remember this night, too. I kept the drapes drawn against the parking lot even though I craved the rush of moonlight. Something about Number Two and the cheap scent of her bar-slut grief fed the fever as I waited in sallow darkness, slowly and fully transforming. By the time she woke, already shackled, the simple whites of her eyes ignited a ravenous fury.

Now, instinct whimpers inside my throat. Fight or flight. I can still feel the teeth savaging through me, still feel the horrors from the last girl. Writhing, shaming, staining. I want to claw the memory from my mind. Chains rattle around my ankle, and the beast's musky feral cravings stink up the night. I make the mistake of glancing up, of meeting the yellow eyes beneath the piggy mask with the whites of my own.

"Shall we begin?"

"Wait, you idiot, I'm y—"

The beast pounces, crushing me beneath a greasy blur of twisted flesh and slavering urges. I lash out and resist, a frenzy of desperation before the return of bone-ripping agony. I try to form words to alert myself to myself—to quell the beast—but only screams escape me. These futile limbs I've been cursed to possess, this whimpering female puppet, this moon-crossed body tears apart like soggy tissue paper.

Such inevitable savagery, such a tragic sinking black-winged escape. Fighting, flailing, nothing is enough. All I can do is scream and gasp and gurgle.

Until all I can do is die.

Number Three—The Hag with the Smeared Lipstick

Waking, I jerk upright in an antique bed, ringing a heavy dinner-bell of chains. My wrists thrust backward, already locked to Number Three's headboard. A third chain encircles my ankles and snakes off the bed. I know to look for danger in the inky corner by the window, even before my age-blurry eyes adjust to the shadow-edged moonlight. Messed-up head ghosts and deep-cut scars and an obscene festering helplessness nest inside me. My mouth panics open, frantic to cough up butterfly wings and frail pleas. Fucking hell, I can't endure myself again.

"I know you're there," I cry out in a wheezing dusty voice, *déjà vu* hammering inside this hag's old splinter-bone chest. The damn butterfly haunts the air, unseen, unchallenged. "I know what you want . . ."

I first saw Number Three in the market. The crooked smear of her lipstick, the way it bled into the crow-cracks around her mouth, waxy red gore staining her dentures. This one clung to a beauty that had fled years ago, yet I could still smell the glory inside her. Doesn't matter how old a girl gets, inside they all possess the same lovely meat. That's why I shadowed Number Three home to her lonesome cabin and marked her for the full moon.

Now, the piggy mask tilts its head, raw menace creaking forward from corner shadows, dowsing flesh in nourishing moonlight. "Shall we begin?"

"No, wait, wait! I know you, *I am you!*" And from my inner bile I speak sour words, the long-ago name of the wretched little man who hides inside the beast.

The name I try to forget.

"How the fuck?" The piggy mask looms closer, bare muscles bulging, shackle chains ringing. I remember thinking I heard the old bat wrong.

"Listen, I know what you want with this one." I stroke this body's wrinkled throat and fragile ribcage, shackles straining like this raspy haggard voice. "She reminds you of Mother. Reminds you of all the girls who sensed something off about you, all the girls you could never have. Not unless you chain yourself to them . . ."

"Shut your whore-bitch mouth," the piggy mask growls.

And holy fucking hell, he's right, I sound like one of *them*. A virgin, a whore, an old hag. All these scars, they're warping me. It's not enough to prove myself to myself. The creature I just described could be any lone monster drunk on moonshine. *My* beast tromps closer, through the slanted lunar light. Vertebrae popping into a feral arch, muscles bulging and rippling against fever-greased skin. The jagged shape of his darkness pours over the ceiling then the wall, curling over the bag of wrinkled flesh that holds me hostage.

"The first time the fever touched you," I rasp, truth burning as sour as my own name, "the first time you transformed in the moonlight, you were young, home alone on the farm with the family hog—"

"I said shut up!" The beast explodes outward, flesh flying.

Number Three's agony is worse than the others. The beast draws this one out, takes his brutal time, adding to antique pains. Hoary arthritic body, brittle heartbeat, tattered womanhood, this uppity hag that endured much, witnessed much. Bones and organs and vital core cocooned in a lifetime of scars.

I scream from within myself as they all spill open.

Hideous, hideous, hideous! No man, no stalker, no beast should ever be forced to see inside a woman, to bear her insult like this, to suffer the obscenity of her pain. Never, never, this curse! Wings eclipse the moonlight. I try to warn myself, one final rasping bloody breath.

"The blue moon will get y—"

A reeking, glistening mouth snaps forward and gnaws my tongue from my flapping chasm, jarring my dentures sideways, silencing me as evermore horrors imprint evermore scars. I stare into the perfectly malformed humanity behind those yellow eyes.

And there's no escaping myself.

Even death offers no mercy.

Number Four—The Bitch with the Butterfly Tattoos

I wake without a bed, standing regal and upright before a cobwebbed mirror, smiling into my reflection. Obsidian eyes, a goddess of inked skin and silver piercings. I exist within her, a mind paralyzed inside this endless moon-stained hellscape. I cannot bend this one's flesh to my will, cannot look away. Because I'm not the only one who watches, not the one who pulls the strings. Moonglow glazes the mirror, and the bitch smiles and smiles.

"Hello," she hisses, echoing through my head. "I speak now to the little man inside the big bad devil."

In the blurred periphery of her vision, her bare throat and stoic shoulders twitch with that inky lacework of butterfly tattoos. Velvet wings rise and fall, matching the quicksilver rhythm of a breath I cannot control. Spidery legs tickle across her collarbone, and others emerge from the silken neckline of her nightgown, evermore wings soft with glowing moons, swarming together, becoming legion.

"Those girls will never feel their deaths," the

bitch hisses. "They will never feel the senseless pain you inflicted. But you will, over and over . . . "

All around, dusty wings scratch a growing tempest inside the walls. A crude altar cuts into her bare feet. I feel them, papery and slimy, freshly hatched chrysalises spiraling outward to bind the moonlight.

" . . . over and over, you'll suffer your own carnage until you learn to tame yourself."

Now she drifts from the mirror, taking me with her. Inky butterflies alight the air as she crawls into her bed. Atop the mattress, she lies supine. I feel her smile unhinge as three butterflies swirl downward, creeping inside, feasting on nectar inside her throat.

As the three eggflies gorge on sweet promises of revenge, the bitch with the butterfly tattoos becomes a theater corpse—a perfectly motionless creature of raw feral allure, a spider weaving a web and baiting her trap. I cannot move her, not a limb, not a finger, not a heartbeat, even as I squirm and howl and rage inside the shell of her. How dare she cage the beast! I am a savage! The moonlight is mine! Those girls were mine! I am the Blue Moon Ripper, for fuck's sake! I am the beast divine!

You will see what it is to be divine . . .

The words echo through me, unbidden, as Number Four focuses her wide-open gaze on the twitching, cocoon-shrouded ceiling. Obsidian eyes collecting moondust. Waiting.

Nearby, a window breaks.

Heavy footsteps approach the bed.

A piggy mask leans over me, and shackles rattle around my wrists.

I scream silently inside, and eggflies scrape my teeth. Looking up at myself, into those relentless yellow eyes, I feel my blue moon curse ready to hatch again, around and around in this endless flittering swirl of death. And I wonder if I will ever learn.

The bitch smiles. "Shall we begin?"

GOOP BY GOOP

Interview With Charles Pieper, Writer of Destroy All Neighbors

Lor Gislason

DESTROY ALL NEIGHBORS hit Shudder in January and ever since I've been a bit obsessed with it. Over-the-top gore and goop, a batshit plotline with a dash of heart and humour, and Alex Winter chewing the scenery as Vlad, the neighbor from hell. Charles Pieper wrote the film and was nice enough to put up with my sporadic emails covering a random assortment of topics to do with both the movie and his career.

LOR: How did the script start?

CAP: I started writing *Destroy All Neighbors* ten years ago for my music video director friend Josh Forbes. We both had horrible neighbors, so we pooled our frustrations together into the initial script. And at the time my job was a painter/animator at Gabe Bartalos's FX shop 'Atlantic West Effects.' So Gabe knew of my real deal awful neighbor way back when that was influencing the film he eventually did designs on a decade later!

'Destroy' was actually my second professional collaboration with Gabe; he created puppet effects for a short horror film I wrote and directed called *Malacostraca* several years ago. It has an extremely different tone . . . *Destroy All Neighbors* is a wacky live action cartoon while *Malacostraca* is a very serious psychological clusterfuck, so to say.

(Lor note: Gabriel Bartalos is an SFX artist who's worked on the Leprechaun *film series as well as most of Frank Henelotter films—classic goop right here. I have a soft spot for* Brain Damage.*)*

LOR: They are definitely tonally different, but both deal with real human anxiety through the lens of body horror. Do you think this is one of the strengths of horror?

CAP: Yes, I love how the genre can allow a storyteller to work through real anxieties, be they personal or societal, while also having fun or being wild. Horror is the best for this!

LOR: I love that it was based on real neighbor frustrations. I hope Vlad is exaggerated, because I cannot imagine living next door to someone like that.

CAP: Vlad is exaggerated but honestly not by that much. Vlad in the film is nicer than the real neighbors he was based on; My real neighbor was a cokehead alcoholic who'd play EDM and 80s music all night long while having ragers with weird miscreants. Josh's neighbor was an alcoholic who'd howl and yell through the walls that he wanted to kill Josh's children. So yeah . . . fun times! I lived next to my real neighbor for two and a half years before he finally got evicted, and I was actively writing the earliest drafts of the script while being kept up at night by him. Madness!

LOR: As an EDM enjoyer (often at 2am), I apologize.

CAP: Your apology is accepted, ahaha!

LOR: I find my writing is based on the concept of "wouldn't that be fucked up" or "wouldn't that be funny" and a lot of *Neighbors* reminds me of that. Every outcome is the *worst* possibility, and that adds to the insanity. Am I on the right track here?

CAP: Yeah, Josh and I pooled our real world woes together and cranked them to 11 in terms of "how badly could the worst version of this go"!

LOR: How did Alex Winter and Jonah Ray get involved in the project?

CAP: Alex Winter didn't come on until maybe 9 years into the script's development. My first drafts a decade ago were written before him or Jonah were even attached. Josh reached out to Jonah about two years into our writing process, and he came on board just as a friend with a handshake agreement. The first punch up writer came on at the same time, and it kept slowly evolving (and getting rejected all over Hollywood) for years and years until Jonah finally sent the script to Alex for consideration. There certainly were other actors floated for Vlad across the years but it ending with being played by Alex was perfect.

LOR: Vlad getting beheaded happens pretty quickly (and is in the trailer, so it's not really a spoiler). What kind of rigs did you guys have set up to hide his body? How much of it was practical effects?

CAP: Alex Winter spent a ton of time with his body hidden in fake couches or carved out bathtubs. Or with his head trapped on a shelf and his body in a green suit to get keyed out. The film is about 90 percent practical effects. Of course, there was green screen and digital replacement for the end battle sequence, but everything regarding characters was all entirely practical effects made by Gabe Bartalos and Bill Corso.

LOR: Each neighbor has a very distinct look once they kick the bucket—can you tell me a bit about the design process?

CAP: The design of all the corpse-ghosts were done by the amazing effects artist Gabe Bartalos, and it was important to him that they all have

unique silhouettes and graphically, visually, stand out from each other were they in, say, a police line-up, haha.

LOR: Was it important to you guys to have practical effects vs CGI?

CAP: Having practical effects was very important to Josh and me, and was inherently baked into the way I wrote the script. I knew I always wanted Gabe to work on it, and I am so glad that, a decade later, we had him on board the film!

LOR: I ADORE the intro credits going through all these tunnels of gore and nastiness. Did you have any input on that?

CAP: The stop-motion opening credits yes, that was very much brought in by me . . . The very first draft I ever wrote explicitly stated that the film starts with a wild stop-motion intro credits sequence . . . and that is exactly what ended up in the film! All those tubes/tunnels the camera is flying through are all physical objects, clay, meat, metal, you name it . . . They exist! The animator on that is a real legend; his name is Rich Zim, and he's the best claymation animator in the world in my opinion. Back in the 1990s he animated on *The Nightmare Before Christmas* and *James and the Giant Peach* and a ton more. He is incredible.
This was my second time working with him . . . he did the claymation guts closeups in the animated short *Everybody Goes to the Hospital* that I produced during the quarantine pandemic years.

LOR: Are you working on anything currently? Anything we should keep an eye out for in the future?

CAP: I am currently working on several scripts I am getting out there including a feature version of my short film *Malacostraca*. As for what comes out next, well, only time will tell, but stuff is percolating!

For more on Pieper's work, check out his site, www.charlespieper.com

AN EXCERPT FROM HAUNTED HEARTS

Lucas Mangum

AND NOW, AN EXCLUSIVE EXCERPT OF *HAUNTED HEARTS* BY LUCAS MANGUM, AVAILABLE NOW FROM GHOULISH BOOKS

1

Abiding Glory Cemetery, September 30

We sat on the grass drinking forties while our legs dangled in front of the door to the Meier crypt. Pinprick stars dotted the near-midnight sky. The moon shone silvery through the thinning branches of a nearby elm. A cricket sang a lonely, atonal solo somewhere behind me. In one of the yards across the cemetery, a fire blazed, and I could smell the burning pine. My head buzzed with malt liquor and the hint of vanilla in Greta's perfume. She wore a green sweater and makeup that made her eyes look especially dark after nightfall. She was the only one of our trio who didn't need a nom de plume. Her last name was Graves. How fucking perfect was that? Pumpkin Ghost stood below us,

shifting from foot to foot and puffing on a blunt he'd already smoked half of.

He didn't know about me and Greta, that we'd screwed a week before. The two of them were sort of a thing, but so were the three of us. Eldritch Youth. That was the name of our band, and the reason Greta and I kept quiet about our afternoon together.

That night in the cemetery, we were sort of celebrating.

It was the night before the opening of Kip Creeker's Trail of Terror.

"Where's your sister, dude?" Pumpkin Ghost asked.

"I dunno." I checked my phone. No messages. "She should've been here by now."

"Want to send her a message?" Greta asked.

I shrugged. "Kathleen's coming, too. She always takes forever getting ready."

"Well, she better hurry." Pumpkin Ghost looked at a watch that wasn't there. "Getting close to midnight."

"She'll be here," Greta said.

"Yeah."

Pumpkin Ghost took another hit off the blunt.

We just need to act like it never happened. That's all.

That's what she told me afterward when I felt a panic attack coming on. Sitting beside me now, she seemed so cool, so measured. It seemed like to her it really *had* never happened. My dad said women were good at turning themselves off. He also said they were good at hiding what they felt. He imparted both of these nuggets of wisdom in the years since his divorce from my mom. In the case of Greta, I wasn't sure which was better. If she could really switch off her emotions like my dad said women could, it was definitely better for our band, provided I could get mine under control, too. However, the fact that our tryst weighed on her, that it *meant something*, filled me with a strange excitement.

"Look, a bat!" Greta said, pointing between two trees.

We all looked up and watched it flutter in erratic directions under the moonlight. Pumpkin Ghost laughed.

"So cool," Greta said.

The little creature flew away, and we all went silent. To fill the space, I said, "That was some gas you were spitting tonight, Ghost."

He grew uncharacteristically solemn.

"Always conjuring, always exorcising."

He grinned, but it didn't have the usual brightness.

Does he know?

A car on the road separating Abiding Glory from the Trail of Terror switched off its lights and entered the cemetery gates.

"Cops?" Pumpkin Ghost snuffed the blunt.

"No, it's Jamie," I said.

The car approached up the gravel road. Greta and I jumped down. Pumpkin Ghost followed in a slow shuffle I sometimes thought he practiced. We slid into the backseat, Greta in the middle. The dashboard clock said it was nine minutes to midnight.

Kathleen drove us to the quarry while Jamie couldn't seem to settle on a song to play on the stereo. Pumpkin Ghost typed fragments of lyrics into his phone. I tried not to think about Greta's leg resting against mine, or what it meant.

I tried not to think about what it meant the week before, her showing up at my place and asking if my mom was home, and when I said no, asking if Jamie was, and when I told her Jamie was out with Kathleen, her plunging her slender fingers into my hair. What that meant. Her mouth covering mine, my lips giving way to the pressure of her tongue, the amount of time we stood making out in the doorway before I pulled away, asking why. Her calling my bluff with her hand on my crotch. What it meant, my sudden embarrassment of the unkempt bedroom she'd seen plenty of times before. As friends, I mean. How long had that crushed beer can been sitting on the desk? Did it smell weird?

Are you sure you want to do this?

What it meant, our clothes on the floor and her on top of me, rocking her hips with desperate, feral energy. Fucking me like I'd never been fucked before and like I don't think I'll ever be fucked again for as long as I live. The way she screamed when she came before switching up her rhythm, ensuring I got mine before the panic of my mom or sister coming home could kill my chances.

What it meant when she collapsed on top of me afterwards, that glint in her eyes. Our heavy breathing. How she kissed my chin and said, *Thanks, I needed that,* and how she didn't want to talk about it further, said we should probably pretend it didn't happen.

As if I could think of pretending while still inside of her.

I believe in you, Moon Boy.

In the back of Kathleen's car with our legs still touching, I tried not to think of those perfect dimples at the base of her spine. It took everything in me to not reach for her hand or caress her knee through her black leggings.

The car stopped. Headlights beaming pale across the fence and the patch of evergreens surrounding the quarry. Three minutes to midnight.

The five of us crawled through a hole under the fence Pumpkin Ghost and I had dug when we were fifteen. Kathleen complained about getting dirty, but Jamie coaxed her through, even taking her girlfriend's hand from the other side. The trees swayed in a sudden chill breeze, and I wondered if what we came here to see had already come. I looked toward the quarry. The space above it was dark. I checked my phone.

"Shit," I said.

I showed the others. It was 12:03.

"So, what?" Jamie said. "You think ghosts really care what time it is?"

Kathleen giggled.

"It's not funny," Pumpkin Ghost said. "Certain things, well, they have meaning, you know?"

Kathleen covered her mouth but didn't stop laughing.

"Was it definitely midnight when we saw it?" I asked.

Worth a shot, I figured. It was four years ago after all. Maybe our memory was foggy.

"What, you don't remember? Man, I remember that shit like yesterday."

"It's called the witching *hour,* though, right?" Greta said. "Not the witching *three minutes.*"

"Yeah, but if no one was around to see, maybe it just went back to sleep."

At this, Kathleen burst into laughter again. Jamie tried shushing her, but broke into laughter of her own.

"Let's just check it out," Greta said.

"Yeah, can't hurt," I said.

Pumpkin Ghost shrugged. "Yeah, I guess, just . . . " He looked at Jamie and Kathleen. "Keep it down, okay?"

My sister and her girlfriend dummied up, but couldn't hold it in. Pumpkin Ghost marched ahead, not bothering to check if anyone else followed. Greta and I exchanged glances and went after him. I gestured for Jamie and Kathleen to come, too. A couple paces down the trail, I looked over my shoulder to make sure they had. Jamie gave me a nod. Kathleen had stopped laughing and was taking dainty, careful steps so she could avoid anything that might dirty up her outfit.

The trail was a steep decline, rocky and somewhat overgrown. The quarry had been closed down some decades ago. There were a number of different reasons given. It all depended on who you talked to what reason was the *real* reason. If you had a teacher who was interested in local history, interested enough to dedicate a whole week of classes to it, you might be led to believe a coalition of concerned parents, bolstered by environmental activists, had made a brave stand against the Landry Corporation to preserve an area of land in which kids could be kids and explore nature, a nature allowed to thrive unimpeded by the reach of industrialization. Of course, that didn't explain having a fence around the area, but such questions were discouraged. If you were bold enough to ask your teacher about the fence, you might hear that the place had, for a while, been a paradise, a Garden of Eden where wilderness and youth frolicked together, until one kid died after falling off a cliff, condemning the land. By this point, the Landry Corporation had moved on to other towns with land to exploit, so no one bothered to repeal the preservation bill, and now it just sat, barricaded off, and only explored by the more

daring of our county's youth, which was, of course, all of us. It was a rite of passage.

Some of the men my dad drank with gave a different reason altogether. They said a quarry worker died in a nasty fall. This doomed, unnamed victim of an unsafe working environment happened to leave behind a rich widow who sued the shit out of the Landry Corporation, the county, the state, and maybe even God Himself. The endless litigation perpetrated by a woman no one seemed to know left the quarry fenced-in and overgrown for maybe fifteen, maybe even twenty years. One of my dad's drinking buddies claimed to have worked with the faceless dead man who launched a thousand lawsuits, even claimed to have laid the grieving widow in subsequent years, but he didn't mention any names.

Like most scenarios with multiple parties involved, all with their own special interests, I suspected some of what I heard was true, some of it was bullshit, and some of it was a little of both. Not much of it really resonated with me, truth be told. Nothing except for the third possible reason given for the closure of the quarry. This one was said to originate from Kip Creeker himself, though he didn't seem to want to talk about it whenever anyone asked him. It was the same reason the five of us headed there minutes after midnight on the first of October.

I wasn't sure *haunted* was the right word. As we approached the edge of the pit, I felt on edge myself. I so clearly remembered what Pumpkin Ghost and I saw here that night, but we were high and really *wanted* to see something. What if it never actually happened? I worried about looking stupid in front of Jamie and Kathleen, but mostly in front of Greta. Though she often claimed she believed in the possibilities of the paranormal, she remained skeptical, unlike Pumpkin Ghost who was a true believer and me who was somewhere in the middle. Greta had never been out to the quarry after midnight. She once confided in me that she'd avoided it for so long because she feared it might end up disappointing her.

We came out of the woods and reached the precipice. The vast quarry stretched before us, dark and silent. The opposite side, from what I could tell, looked a lot like our side. Shadows made it difficult to see for sure, but it was another steep drop-off, near lots of trees.

"Fucking told you guys," Pumpkin Ghost said. "These things are delicate, man."

"What exactly are we looking for?" Kathleen said.

"Doesn't matter. It's not here."

"Well, we should at least wait, right?" Greta said.

Jamie and Kathleen looked to Pumpkin Ghost for answers. He talked like someone who knew what he was talking about and that made people expect him to know things.

"I think we should," I said. "I mean, we just got here. Maybe we need to open ourselves up, relax."

"Do you have any more weed?" Greta asked.

Pumpkin Ghost shook his head. "Yeah, but back at my house."

"We have some," Jamie said. "You guys want to smoke?"

"That wasn't exactly what I had in mind," I said.

"It might not be a bad idea, though," Greta said. "It could set the mood."

"I don't know," I said. Weed had a tendency to make me panicky and weird. Being in the quarry in the middle of the night, trying to see ghosts with the friend who didn't know I'd fucked his girlfriend, I didn't need much help with that.

"Come on," Greta said. She took hold of my forearm and gave it a light squeeze. "It will be okay."

"All right," Jamie said. "I'll pack a bowl."

As if on command, Kathleen dug a baggie of the good stuff out of her purse's inside zipper compartment. According to Jamie, Kathleen got shit from her cousin in Colorado. They came in the hollowed pages of books, inside toy cars, and once, taped inside a ukulele. It was potent stuff, Jamie always testified, which worried me even more.

But Greta's hand on me steered my judgment. I couldn't look weak in front of her. Not now. I nodded as my sister packed a bowl.

When we were all good and high, we sat on the ledge and waited.

"This is so dumb," Kathleen said, and crossed her arms. Jamie elbowed her in the ribs. "What?"

Pumpkin Ghost had a distant look in his eyes as he stared across the chasm. Perhaps he was willing the apparition to show itself. Or perhaps he was contemplating confronting Greta and me later

because he suspected something. I hoped it was only the former.

Greta let her legs dangle, the only one of us brave enough to do so. I wasn't afraid of heights or anything. I just didn't like the idea of letting any part of me hang over a pit so dark and deep. Anything could be down there. Staring into the inky shadows, I could picture skeletal hands reaching up from the depths, flesh hanging off their fingers and wrists in desiccated flaps. Glowing green eyes staring back at me. Unseen, gnashing teeth fiending for teenage flesh like a smoker craves nicotine.

Greta had her hands between her knees and an expectant expression on her face. Her dark eyes staring, her auburn hair draped over her shoulders and down her back, her face flushed with intoxication. She looked so fucking cool to me then. Enigmatic. Even if Eldritch Youth never went on to do anything, I was confident she would. I supposed Pumpkin Ghost would go on to do things, too. His groupies and aspiring rappers who wanted to be him comprised healthy portions of our following. I was only unsure of myself. I didn't have fans—people hardly knew who I was. My stage presence was confined to standing behind my equipment going beep-beep-beep. It didn't matter that my work was the backbone of our compositions, an impressionistic canvas on which the others could express themselves. I needed the others for me to be fully realized; Pumpkin Ghost and Greta could each be fully realized under any circumstances, with anyone providing the space. It didn't need to be me—it only happened to be.

Greta was right: Pumpkin Ghost couldn't find out about us. We had to pretend it never happened, even though by then I'd convinced myself it meant so much.

I closed my eyes and opened them again when Kathleen screamed.

At the edge of the quarry, Kathleen was thrashing her arms and crying out. Her legs buckled like half-deflated tube men. Jamie held onto the hysterical Kathleen to prevent her from falling over the edge, but my sister appeared to be no more than a scared child herself. Pumpkin Ghost tried to conceal his laughter as this ghostly reappearance brought back bad memories which rendered me immobile. Greta stood, pulling her feet from the chasm, never taking her eyes from the rising, pale shape.

We all saw the house—I knew that right away—but Greta saw *inside* the house, just as *I* saw inside the house that night with Pumpkin Ghost four years prior. I could tell because she did the same thing I had done.

She reached out and took a step forward, then another, her foot hovering over the cliff, her torso teetering at the edge of oblivion.

I screamed and reached for her, the way Pumpkin Ghost had reached for me. I wrapped my arm around her waist and pulled her away, and then she was screaming like Kathleen, and I wondered if Kathleen had seen inside as well. I kept pulling Greta back, but she offered no surrender. She fought me with everything she had as she attempted to charge toward inevitable doom. I had to snake another arm around her and yell for Pumpkin Ghost to stop laughing and help me. He grabbed her around the shoulders, and we tackled her to the ground.

"No," she screamed. "No! We have to help her!"

Kathleen's screams became sobs. Jamie held her tighter.

Pumpkin Ghost had quit laughing and now his eyes were wide, showing a rare fear. Greta's resistance slowed and softened.

I looked across the quarry once more.

The house was no longer there.

MY WEREWOLF IN BIO

TT Madden

BRYAN EARL WHITE, 19, has been radicalized. He doesn't realize it, but that's exactly what has happened to him. Of course, radicalized people never know it's happening to them. They think it's everyone else who's the problem. Bryan isn't indoctrinated in the pulpit, like his mother was in her youth, watching shrieking sermons from a man who claimed to be channeling divinity, who handled snakes and lay hands upon his parishioners.

No, Bryan becomes indoctrinated the twenty-first century way, from behind a keyboard, reading endless unmoderated 4chan comments and watching YouTube videos with staggeringly-long runtimes entitled things like *They Are Sheep(le), But You Are a Wolf*, and *I Will Teach You How to Be an Alpha Male*.

Bryan's favorite influencer is a man named Jordan Voss. This is not the man's human name, though Bryan does not question it in the same way he doesn't ever call The Duke *Marion* instead of *John*, or the guy in all those car movies *Mark* instead of *Vin*, even though he refuses to refer to Elliot Page by his real name.

From Jordan Voss's first video, Bryan knows he's the one for him. Voss' shirt was already off, and he was more muscular than Bryan could ever hope to be. Of course, Bryan could always work out. He had the time. But instead, even though his home state of Florida blocked PornHub, he spent too much of that time jerking off to gangbang porn featuring women who he didn't consciously realize reminded him of his mother; a mom-bod that had clearly seen a kid or two, long, dark hair, brown eyes. His favorite video features a woman with a tiny, silver cross around her neck, the only item that stayed on her person after the five Black guys working on her pool thought she needed to relax a little bit instead of being so wound up about the kids' soccer game or the PTA meeting or whatever the hell was going on, Bryan had just been scrubbing through looking for the good stuff. They all ended up coming inside her one way or another, and Bryan had not a single conscious thought about how maybe he should unpack that.

In Jordan Voss' video, something equally graphic happens; he reaches with both hands behind his back, like he's going to pull off an invisible shirt, but instead grabs a handful of his own skin. Bryan tenses as Jordan whips an entire layer of skin off himself, like it's a hoodie about to go into the hamper, exposing a furred torso underneath, matted with blood and coagulate. The skin doesn't come away in one piece, leaves chunks in places, patches still clinging to Jordan's face and neck and chest. He peels these off quickly, flicking them away, distracting as they are from the overall image of the huge humanoid wolf now taking up the majority of the frame. Jordan shakes himself, just like a dog would, flicking off the blood and slime and bits of skin, and he looks at the camera, at Bryan, and tells him that he, too, can become an alpha. Just like Jordan. All he has to do is like and subscribe, to follow him for more, so that Jordan can tell him how to do it himself.

On some level, Bryan knows YouTube should've blocked Jordan's videos. A truly excessive amount of blood and gore is on display with each horrifying transformation. At first he scrubs through, trying to see if what he saw was some illusion, finding the most-played section of the video to watch the transformations again and again. Endless loops of Jordan tearing his own skin off to expose the wolf underneath, shedding the useless human suit in a symbol of his ascension beyond Man.

But then Bryan starts to actually listen to what Jordan says, falling right into the intricate web of YouTube videos and Spotify podcasts and algorithm recommends that leads him to other wolfed-out influencers who eat ungodly amounts of raw meat that should surely kill them, but maybe not because maybe there's something about a wolf's intestinal tract that's different? Men who tell him he has to come in a woman whenever–if ever–he has sex, because sex was for procreation and only procreation, and if he enjoyed it he might be gay somehow. There are dozens of men who burst at the seams, wolf-jaws tearing into hunks of bloody meat. Guys who film videos sitting in easy chairs complaining about the woke mob that make them look like bargain-bin supervillains from the days of Adam West's *Batman*. Stand-up comedians long past their prime.

All of these men post videos of themselves transforming into monstrous wolves, alphas, ripping off their clothes and their skins, some of them entire full-body shots where Bryan can see their enormous wolf-dicks dangling down between their legs and he thinks *man if I was like these guys I could get a big dick like that and maybe stick it in a girl instead of my fist like maybe that Mallory girl from calc oh fuck yeah!* before he watches the same gangbang video again.

Mallory, the girl from calc, is a *woman*, not a girl. She looks like his mother too, though Bryan doesn't realize that. To him, he just thinks she's an older woman who's gone back to college. He's fantasized about her a million times; fucking her in their classroom, bent over a desk, on the hood of a speeding car. Action hero, alpha shit. In none of those fantasies does he ever imagine paying any actual attention to her, never thinks of asking her what *she* wants or needs, or what she might like. And now with those videos rotting his brain, his fantasies are just more of the same, except in all of them he's a werewolf.

Bryan has no earthly idea what Mallory is actually like because the only time he ever spends with her has been between the hours of ten and eleven fifteen, Monday, Wednesday, and Friday, and even then it's to her eight o' clock, just barely in her peripheral. To him, she exists not as a person, but as an *idea* of a person. Had he ever bothered to get to know her, he would have known she does, in fact, have children. Two. Tommy, 7, and Jessica, 15. That Mallory herself is thirty-seven, and that she gave birth to Jessica when she herself was twenty-two, but now she's finally going back to school after decades of working odd jobs. Bryan would have known Mallory's partner's name is Kyle, or that even though they've begun questioning their gender, have begun using the dreaded pronouns that so many people on Bryan's internet fear, they still refer to themself as Tommy and Jessica's father. He would have known Kyle and Mallory have been together for twenty years, although never married, and that they compare themselves to Kurt Russell and Goldie Hawn in that way. Their life isn't movie-star glamorous, but it's everything either of them ever wanted. Or that her last name is Oswald. Or any one of nine million facts about her actual life that were incompatible with his imagination of her.

Like the fact that she has dealt with men like him before.

Men *just* like him.

Bryan thinks of none of this. None of these things even enter into his mind as possibilities, driven as he is by his need to become an alpha just like Jordan. So he follows the man's instructions, does everything he can to become a werewolf; drinking rainwater out of the footprint of a wolf, sleeping outside on a summer night with the moon shining directly on his face. He spends all his money on a belt made of wolfskin, and even special salves and formulas to drink or rub on his body (paid directly to Jordan Voss' storefront, of course) that taste and smell like bathwater but it doesn't matter if it works.

Bryan has no idea where he could possibly find Satan to make an allegiance with him, which is another way to become a werewolf, but it doesn't come to that, thankfully. One night he feels it, the urge growing strong in his belly. He doesn't know which method actually worked but it doesn't matter as soon as he begins tearing himself apart, ripping his own skin off and throwing chunks of it across his room, his face and shoulder and arm and hand making wet splat sounds as they hit the walls and floor and then he's free, running like a beast howling at the moon and feeling everything he'd ever felt bottled up finally unleashed like one endless orgasm.

He runs and runs and finds a scent he recognizes but can't really remember because he's not driving anymore, some other part of him is, and that part is an animal. An animal with a need. Or at least something that he has convinced himself is a need. He's convinced himself it is something he is owed, something that's his right as a man to take. So he runs, following the scent, his dick already engorged, already rarin' to go and then all of a sudden he's swept up and something has his ankle and it's yanking him up up up and he's swinging, dangling there.

Caught in a fucking pig snare.

They come out of the woods. The shapes. All wearing maroon coats, all looking up at him, all pulling knives and crossbows–*fucking crossbows what is this?*–from underneath those coats and ponchos.

And leading them is Mallory.

Mallory looks up at Bryan, but not in the way he wanted it. He wanted her on her knees, begging him, asking him for more, wondering if she could handle everything he had, but instead his flaccid dick dangles down onto his belly like a shrimp and he swings to and fro, helpless, caught like an animal. A helpless animal.

The Mallory who sits in his calc class. The Mallory who, had he bothered to learn anything about her, has dealt with men like him before, has experience with these supposed alphas. The Mallory who lost a brother to the very same alpha brainrot, who had to put him down in the shed out back like this was Old Yeller. The Mallory, and so many other women, whose goal, as she pulls a silver dagger, is Jordan Voss and all the other alphas like him.

REMEMBER TO FORGET ME

Violet

I TOOK IT WELL, I swear. I didn't even cry or anything. Not this time. When Jocelyn broke up with me? I just nodded along. I mean, I asked her why was she doing this, and did she really mean it, and all that. I asked, Is there anything I can do? I want to fight for you. Tell me how to fight for you. But when she said no, I nodded. Told her that it was okay, that I understood. Sometimes, good things fall apart. Sometimes, the best thing you've ever had—the best thing *either* of you have ever had, in all these years of trying—just falls apart. Even though she used to say that it feels like you've always known each other, like you were girls next door, and everyone said you were perfect together, June and Jocelyn, J and J—sometimes, even *that* falls apart. And it's no one's fault, and you can't do anything about it, at all, ever. You have to forget it and move on.

And that's what I did. I *promise* you, that's exactly what I did. I told her I'd miss her, and I grabbed up my purse and my jacket, and I asked if I could give her one last hug, and I whispered a goodbye in her ear. I told her right then and there—well, the words don't matter.

She didn't listen anyway.

And then I got in my car, and I turned the radio on, rolled onto 287, and went straight home. And that was it.

I took it well. It's not my fault if *she* couldn't get to sleep that night, and it's certainly not my fault if she called me at two in the morning like a complete psycho, screaming at me like Oh, June, did you leave a tape in my house? Did you, like, hack my Bluetooth speaker, or something? I can hear your voice in the walls. Oh, not funny, June, god dammit, June, I have to *work* in the morning, can you just tell me where it is? I told her so many times that I had no *idea* what she was talking about, and there was no way I could've done anything—I mean, did I even leave the room for a *second* while I was over there? Even to use the bathroom? No. Because she wanted to get right down to business, she wanted to sit me on the couch and tell me how it was, how we just weren't right for each other anymore, or whatever. Point being: how could I have left a tape? How could I have even known to *bring* a tape? I mean, I showed up with Viagra and a tin of Altoids in my purse, that's how *I* thought the night was going to go. I didn't know she was going to break up with me. Even if I had, who owns a tape recorder in this day and age? Do I *look* like I know how to hack a speaker?

I tried to explain all that to her, even asked what I was supposedly saying on this tape. And she was all, Oh, like you don't already know, oh, I didn't expect this from you, June, oh, I'm so hurt. Like a martyr. Like *she* wasn't the one who broke up with *me*. And finally, I mean *finally*, when she did just shut up and hold the phone out to her room for me to listen? There was *nothing* there. Nothing at all. Not even a whisper.

So, yeah. She was *not* doing great.

And it's not my fault, either, if she was seeing things the next day. I mean, that's the only sense I can make of it. Her story is that she saw me in her *mirror*. Like, she was brushing her teeth alone at that chipped bathroom sink—which, since I wasn't in her life anymore, I'm sure was stained with flat soda and loose hairs and little flecks of stubble and probably had all her pill bottles lined up right on the edge, finasteride and estrogen and SSRIs, with all the lids off so they could spill *right* down the drain if they tipped over—and looked up, and saw me standing behind her, naked, *smiling*. And, like, honestly? When I heard about that, it made me feel *good*. I know it shouldn't have, I know it sounds like *I'm* the crazy one, but *I* know I wasn't there, and that means she was seeing things, and *that* means she wasn't as over me, as *out of love* with me, as she thought. It had felt so *sudden,* our breakup—out of the blue, like had she even thought it through? And honestly, I don't think she did. She hadn't thought it through, and now she was feeling bad for it.

Which—that's not to say I'm happy about everything else that happened. Obviously. I never wanted to be the straw that broke her back, or whatever, but secretly, *privately*, I was glad that she was struggling, because it meant that I had *mattered* in some way. And I'm not proud of myself for feeling happy, but I did. Wouldn't you? Deep down, at least?

But the point is, she was already losing it. If you saw her house, you'd get what I mean—there's not even space for me to have stood behind her at the sink, not unless we were skin-to-skin. It backs right up against the shower, and she always pulls the curtain shut as soon as she gets out because she says the stink from the toilet gets in there otherwise. (I don't get it, either.) I'm sure her roommate told her that, too. Like, Um, Jossie, what's the *deal* with you, there's, like, no way she was there, alright, sweetie? Maybe you, just, like, need some rest, or whatever? You're probably just, like, all sad about her, or something? You should, like, totally take stock of your mental health, you know?

Because—here's the other thing—it's not like she didn't have a *reason* to snap. Her sob story (I mean, *her* specific sob story, aside from just being trans) was about this car wreck she got into one summer years ago. She always pretended she was happy about it—*my happy little car accident,* she called it, because what happened was, she was drunk driving and she clipped this other car's fender changing lanes and spun out and hit a guardrail, and a chunk of her Subaru's frame went right through her groin, and when she woke up in the hospital, she had a vagina. She was midway through transitioning, and her penis was all torn up from the crash, and she had talked to her doctor about getting bottom surgery eventually, and they weren't going to be able to save it anyway, so they gave her a fresh new pussy. And right after that, she quit drinking, she came out to her family, and she changed her name from Jonathan to Jocelyn. (Sorry, should I not have *said* Jonathan? You'll probably get all pissed at me, like her deadname's a dirty word now, right? Sure, just *pretend* she never had that name, *ignore* it, you're such a fucking saint. She's not here. She probably wouldn't even mind, not *really*.)

So, yeah. *Happy little car accident.* Just, I think it'd be absolutely traumatic, getting in a wreck like that. Call it what you want, but wouldn't you think it'd fuck you up? Everything changing like that, all at once? That was the old me, she would say—the drinking, and the internalized transphobia, and the penis, all that icky stuff in her past, it was the *old* her. This was the *new* her, brand new and shiny, overnight. That's when she started needing all those pills, I bet. After the crash.

And you know what? It's not my fault if she *didn't* take care of herself, if she *didn't* take her meds and get some rest after her little *hallucination*. It's not my fault if she pulled ten hours at the restaurant that day and decided she needed to unwind, I mean *really* unwind, when she got home. Because, listen: like I said, she was slipping. I mean, I love her. I hate her, too, but I love her, and as angry as I got, I also know that what she did next . . . it wasn't like her.

What *was* like her, though, was throwing back an edible or, sometimes, some mushrooms after a long shift, because even if she'd quit drinking, she always saw herself as that punk hippie chick. Maybe once a month, she'd meet up with me after her shift on a Saturday and she'd be blazed, eyes the size of the moon, laughing about every little thing and zoning out whenever the music came on. Or we'd get together on a Sunday and we'd trip together, and she'd say—she'd say—shit, I'm sorry, I just *miss* her. She'd say . . . that it was almost like she was remembering me from out of time, like we'd been together before we ever met. Like we'd been through all of this before. I know I shouldn't be crying, I *know*, I'm *pathetic*. I'm sorry. But she'd say things like that, and sometimes it was beautiful, you know? But sometimes . . . sometimes, with mushrooms, you just have a bad trip. There was someone else on the pavement, she told me one time, and I knew she meant during that crash. There was someone else, the paramedics didn't help him. They ignored him. She couldn't stop dwelling on it, which is why I *know* it was eating at her all the time, I *know* she wasn't okay. She was imagining things. She never brought up that other person before or since, and believe me, it's not the kind of thing you forget, seeing death. I think the drugs were bad for her, is what I'm trying to say. She couldn't handle them.

It's the only thing that makes sense. So it must be true.

It's not my fault if she decided to work all day, and then decided to eat a bunch of shrooms, and wound up hearing my voice again and calling me at half past eleven, crying for me to leave her alone. It's not my fault if she thought she saw someone who looked like me standing outside (still naked, erect, smirking) and called the cops, and yelled at them when they told her that nobody was there. Because *nobody was there.* I was heartbroken, but I never would've stalked her. Not like that.

And it's *definitely* not my fault if she started seeing things that *no way* could've happened. You know—if she saw me looking at her from inside her TV screen, watching her watching me. If she panicked and closed Netflix, but I was still there, scowling from the Roku home screen, eyes turning violet and red, blood dripping from my mouth, or something. If she heard my voice say, *You'll never be rid of me*, and took that as some kind of challenge, and grabbed a lamp off the side table and threw it into the TV, shattered that glass, knocked the whole screen straight off the wall. That big, expensive TV that her roommate had just bought, and now was coming out of her room to look at, to scream over, like Um, what the fuck did you, like, do that for, Jossie? Are you, like, on your meds? Because this (waving her fingernails) is some, like, *testosterone*-heavy shit, okay? That thing was, like, my prized possession, or whatever.

And—this is why I brought up the drugs—it's not my fault if they couldn't deal with the situation like reasonable adults. If they got to arguing, and the roommate said, Um, sweetie, I know you're all, like, totally whacked over this girl, but you're kinda being a bitch, you know? You're, like, having a psychotic break or something, you know? And that hit a nerve, and Jocelyn was like, Oh, it's not about June, oh, she doesn't matter to me, what matters is that you used the wrong words! Oh, I'm not crazy, don't call me crazy! Oh, why'd you bring up testosterone, that's so *wrong* of you, I'm on estrogen like a *real* woman, oh, who even *cares* about June?

If she got in her roommate's face. If her roommate started fishing for the Mace, and if Jocelyn picked up the lamp again, like a weapon, if they almost came to blows and finally had to just walk away from each other, like *wow*, that was close, can you believe us? If, as she was turning away, she *thought* she saw me in the reflection on the window, sneaking up from behind, with, I don't know, some kind of knife in my hand, or whatever. And, I mean—even if I *were* there, isn't that extreme, the way she acted? It could've been a butter knife, or something that *looked* like a knife but was really a bit of tinfoil, or the glint off a phone screen. That's why I think she must've been tripping, because even if I had been there, it would've been an overreaction to heft that lamp up, and spin around, and *thwack* it full-force into whatever happened to be behind her—which, because I *wasn't* there, was her roommate's thick skull—with enough force to shatter bone and throw chunks of grey-green brain all over the walls. Is it cliche to call it a Jackson Pollock, yet? You know, when it's blood and not paint streaking down, when it's bits of muscle and thin yellow fluid stringing the splotches together, when there's maybe even one blue eyeball that gets knocked free and drips to the floor, staring back up like to tell you, Hey, maybe splatter painting isn't for everyone, but I guess beauty's in the eye of the beholder?

It's not my fault if she was so *gone*, by that point, that she did all this. *She* broke up with *me*, let's not forget—she shouldn't have done that without a self-care plan, without *something* to make sure she didn't snap.

And, I mean, say you *do* buy Jocelyn's story, her batshit crazy story, the one that blames everything on *me*, like fucking *always*. Say that, as she was on her knees, shaking, not even crying because how could any of this have *happened*, how could she *deserve* to cry when she'd just committed a fucking *murder*, her roommate's fingers really *did* twitch.

Say that the corpse let out a low sound, like its last breath was only now draining away, and then . . . *moved*, barely at all but all at once, this sort of ripple passing through all those dead muscles.

Say that she looked at the bits of shattered TV screen on the floor, and saw the glass shards embedded in her roommate's flesh, and put it together that in this mad little world of hers, I *had* been in the TV, and now I was getting *out*. Say that the body drew in one rattling, bone-chilling breath, air scraping into its lungs like raw fiberglass, and pushed itself, inch by inch, up off the floor. Misfit bones popping in their joints. Misfit muscles twitching under misfit skin. Brains sloshing out of the caved-in skull, blood running like tears from an empty socket, loose jaw clicking wetly with each movement. Say that when it turned to face her, the one remaining eye *had* gone bright green, like mine (and, let me point out, like *hers*). I'll admit, I can't explain that part, the eye changing colors. Maybe it had to do with the trauma when the skull exploded, you know, like blood vessels bursting, or something? I mean, there has to be a reason, because I wasn't there, inhabiting that corpse—obviously. That's impossible.

But even if, somehow, I *had* been there—*even then*!—it still wouldn't have been my fault.

It wouldn't have been my fault that she screamed and went straight out the door without even checking her pockets and panicked when she got to the driveway and realized she'd left her keys inside. Or if the corpse of her roommate jumped through the window (not because she had to, but because it would scare Jocelyn and there's no better time to break bones than when they're someone else's) and snarled at her, and she tore off running down the street. If I were Jocelyn, *I* certainly wouldn't have run *toward* the highway, either, but then, it's not like *any* of her decisions in the last couple days were making a *ton* of sense. And it sure as *hell* wouldn't be my fault if, when the zombie finally scuttled fast enough to catch up to her—not wanting to *kill* her, mind you, just to, I don't know, catch her, hold her close, and, like, pin her to the ground and scrape her scalp against the pavement and make her say I love you, make her *admit* I love you I love you I love you and that's why I can never let you go, or something—and dived, hooked one claw-like finger into the rolled-up hem of her skinny jeans, and pulled *just* hard enough to tangle her feet and make her spill out onto the shoulder of 287, headlights roaring past in the night, she only just *then, finally*, after *all this time*, looked into that green eye and recognized it.

If she realized, way too late for either of us, that *yeah*, she *had* known me before. That she had been in this place before. That there *had* been someone else out there on the pavement with her, *dying*, someone that she and the rest of the world had *ignored*—a ghost being born, a reflection, a memory of the girl she never said goodbye to, trapped in all that shattered glass.

That June was for John, and for the month of the crash, the month her deadname died.

If, realizing this, she screamed her throat raw. If she decided that the *very best way* to end this haunting was to *throw me*

head over heels, fingers still hooked around her ankle so tight they pulled meat from bone

into the hood of a speeding Subaru

and I smacked spiderwebs into the windshield, and the car swerved left, then right, and then clipped the fender ahead of it and spun out and slammed into the guardrail with enough force to shatter steel and snap bones and tear the driver's womanhood away from her—*if* all of this happened, it wouldn't be my fault.

It wouldn't be my fault, because she's done this all before, and she *keeps getting it wrong*. Because she *deserves* this—because she *wouldn't fucking love me*, and when she told me we were through, I told her she had to *mean* it, I told her I would *fight* for her, I *told* her the way out, and she *didn't fucking listen*. Because all I am is what she gave me: the worst parts of herself. Because I whispered in her ear before I left:

remember to forget me.

On a hot summer night, something enormous screams down from the sky and pierces into the desert not far from the small town of Farchapel. The stories that trickle back from the crater are strange indeed—those who find it and return claim to be forever changed, transformed into the better, ideal versions of themselves they've always wished to achieve.

Jamie, recent mysterious visitor in town, is a man on the run, all too eager to escape his current form no matter the cost. Sidney, local drunk, would rather face a hole in the ground than the things he's done. As the two men venture into the desert canyons in search of their better selves, they soon discover that what hides there is much more terrible—and eager to lure them in.

WWW.GHOULISH.RIP

SWERVE

Perry Meester

HE WANTS TO know why they do it. Sometimes they're still alive when he gets there, too stubborn to be annihilated outright and too maimed to crawl off into the woods, their stick-frail bodies bent a hundred different ways. Those times Russ has to put them out of their misery right there on the side of the road. It comes with the public works job—someone's gotta do it.

And people hit a lot of deer.

The *why* bothers him more than the mess. *It jumped right out in front of me,* some crying mom will say, her kids huddled around her, trying to peer back at the body. Last week a crying teenager clutched her phone against her chest and blinked without any tears at all, while the tow truck lurched behind her. *I came around the corner and it just stood there, it just stood there, it wouldn't move, it didn't get out of the way.*

It was dark. I didn't see it. It didn't move.

Headlights confuse them; the roar of the cars sends them into a frenzy. Their tiny deer brains hit panic mode and throw them in whichever direction occurs to them first. Sometimes while he scrapes flesh off the road Russ sees luckier ones cross up ahead. They're fast enough, graceful enough, to be smarter than this. Their wide eyes when they stop before disappearing into the trees always grab him. He drives slow in the early mornings on the way to work and keeps eyes on the tree line for any tawny flashes. In his bed at night they clop-clop-clop through the dark. Stupid motherfuckers. All that

shyness and they always end up in front of cars, where the ambulance won't come for *them.*

So—just this one night, he doesn't drive so cautious on his way home. He makes it to 60 going past the yellow glare of a sign cautioning drivers to slow to 35. In the seconds before he hits her, Russ is grinning, body leaning into the curve, head bobbing with the thrashing music, feeling the ton-and-a-half structures around him threaten to abandon the parkway entirely and disappear off the mountain slope on the other side of the guardrails.

The doe is there when he starts to level out. She steps from the black smear of trees and into the center of the lane, eyes afire. She blinks while the animal panic in Russ' skull makes him lay on the horn, slam on the brakes. When her lithe body cracks against the windshield, he's sure he hears her laugh, high and gleeful.

The truck skids perpendicular, blocking both lanes. The air is burnt rubber, animal hair, the rich earth and mountain. Before his breathing stutters and flails too bad to think straight, Russ clicks on his hazards. Seems like the sensible thing to do.

How often has he thought about this?

Disconnected from the aux, phone speakers wail a shitty guitar solo, lost somewhere behind a seat. Adrenaline sharpens the edges of the world. His heart skitters horribly. Inches from his face, the doe's head lolls in through a crack in the glass. Her tongue hangs from her shattered jaw as she watches him, dripping a thin stream of blood onto the emergency brake. A sound like air escaping a balloon whines from deep inside her.

"Oh," Russ says.

Nothing in her rolling eyes has anything to say

about her reasons. Deer are always smaller than you'd think, once you see them up close, and she's as small as an adult might get; maybe enough to be malnourished. She flinches when he reaches past her for his phone.

He is unsurprised when the words NO SIGNAL greet him. This deep into the mountains and the park cell service is a gift. As he cuts off the music, the air around them dampens, goes thick with chirping insects, rustling wind. The deer pants. Outside his steady circle of blinking yellow lights there is nothing. Trees in every direction, the road winding ahead, all felt, not seen, crushing closer.

Russ slides out of the truck an inch at a time, testing for anything that feels broken. Emptiness is better than the stink of the animal filling up the interior. Her hot breath is meaty. Like her relatives festering in the sun before he gets to them. Her fur radiates the stench of illness and decay. Some deer are fucked before the car ever hits them.

He took the job a year ago, two years ago, doesn't matter, the days all fade when you work on call. Easy money, if you live by the parkway and you don't mind the mess. Though lately he's been dreaming about it—sometimes even while he's awake. The doe's smell is an old friend.

His phone flashlight sweeps across the damage, where glass and plastic glitter up from the rod. The hood crumples inward. Something goes *click click click* while something else leaks. The doe's back legs scrabble weakly against wreckage. Harsh white bone sticks out from her blood-matted fur. She's stuck neck-deep in that windshield, where the shattered glass traps her where she's vulnerable. Couldn't have happened worse.

"Jesus fuck," Russ is saying, only he doesn't want to say it too loud, on account of the darkness around him, whatever's just outside his limited line of sight. In the park you hear things. Hear about them. You don't go out in the dark. You don't follow noises or calls. You don't attract attention to your lonely little self.

"Why the fuck would you do that?" he asks. "Fuck me."

Inhale, exhale. The doe can't angle her head to look back at him, can only dribble onto the passenger seat, but for what feels like an hour Russ watches her broken neck twitch like she's trying. Bile rises to the back of his throat. She won't live.

She shouldn't. In the back of his truck is his bolt gun and his gloves and his walkie, crucially, and every breath she takes is raw misery, and by the time he can untangle her from the glass safely to get her head against the road there's a good chance she'll have bled out and solved the problem.

"I don't get it," he says, somewhere around the roaring in his ears, while he makes a wide circle to get to the back of the truck. "Don't get it. You can see. You can see the lights. Just get out of the fucking way."

Keys in his pocket. Keys in his hands. Keys in the box to get out the tools. Sanitized after a hard day's work and all in their place. Gloves that fit him perfect. He shrugs into the safety vest more out of habit than duty.

The doe *thuds* against the hood.

Calm, steady. It's one thing when the road is full of emergency lights and another when you're all alone and that's the only real sound around. "Hey. I'm coming."

She has no way to see or know the shape of the gun in his hand. When he comes around, though, she tries again, kicking outward, only succeeding in lifting her body an inch before it falls. Blood leaks from her throat where sharp edges dig in. Russ swallows, hard. The aches and bang-ups from the crash have started to hit. Maybe that's why his head throbs the way it does.

"No way you don't know it's trouble," Russ says. "You wanna tell me why?"

The doe screams. Which he's heard before, of course, that high-pitched bleating noise, wobbling in her throat, devolving into coughs and splutters somewhere in her injured lungs. Something like a little kid blowing into a harmonica. It makes his scalp tingle and his spine itch. It makes something in the woods outside his flashlight beam rustle. She cries for help, and she cries worse when he puts a hand on her. Skin and bones, this one. *Sick.* Bad news. Call-in-for-backup bad news. But leaving her like this feels worse.

Normally there's a second pair of hands to help. Even with the gloves, getting her out of the car means half-crawling onto the hood, avoiding her thrashing and wailing, flinching away from hot metal and hoping something in that engine don't burst. Russ sweeps away the excess glass to make the way for her. He keeps his mouth shut tight while he works because whatever questions he had are gone now, not like she'll answer, and it was *stupid* to hit her, anyway, like the buzzing in his head meant something, like it would be different than any other time. They'll laugh him out of the job. They'll fire him for wrecking the truck. The blood on his hands and shirt smells as bad as it does on the asphalt.

The impulse toward tenderness is gone. As soon as he's knocked enough glass from around her head, he slides off the truck, grabs her by the back legs, and pulls until she hits ground. She falls awkward, on her side, and something inside of her snaps something awful. She whines and sobs.

"Waste of time," Russ offers, by way of condolences. "Maybe one of you'll learn better. Hold on."

Can't hold the bolt gun with thick gloves. Can't work the safety or the trigger in his chilled fingers. Cold out here tonight, up on the mountain, and still as anything. The chill in the back of his neck tells him not to turn around. Don't want to see the eyes lined up looking from the trees, glowing against his hazards.

She's so, so still. Safe enough to approach, though her eyes roll into the whites when he kneels next to her. She barely breathes when he cradles her head in one hand and lines up the bolt. Right through the top of the skull, down into the brain. It'll make her stop. It'll make her stop *crying*.

"Thanks for nothing," Russ says. The anger is seething through him now. At the deer, which is easier than being angry at himself. "Okay—"

The doe stands. He feels her shift in his hand when she does it. Her head slips from his grasp buttery-smooth, her broken neck grinds and clicks, her wobbly legs take her up from the ground into a tottering pile. The shock of it knocks Russ flat on his ass. She blubbers against the pain of every movement, and she looks *right at him right fuckin' at him* down at him with scorn and fire, and she laughs in his face before she waddles off into the trees.

An owl calls. The doe's crashing through the woods fades into the hum of the night. Russ jumps to his feet—he makes it four or five steps before catches himself running after her, down the incline of the mountain. Into deadfalls, rivers, bobcats, and the steady-sure realization that if he goes down that slope, he will find things he does not want to find. The prey animal in the back of his skull hollers that louder than the deer.

Instead, he runs up the safety of the road, past rusted signs for tourists. He does not look back.

***

A middle-aged woman sits outside the service station, sucking on a cigarette beneath her logoed cap. Skin stretches tight and weathered across her hands. In the flickering fluorescents that stretch over four ancient gas pumps she's a mythical creature, pink-striped stringy ponytail and all. Russ wants to fall at her feet. Instead, he picks up into an awkward jog as she watches him approach, aware of his loud breathing and the squeak of his shoes. It's been a while since he's walked a few miles. It's been never since he's done it in the dead of night.

Stacey, the letters on her plastic nametag starting to peel, barely blinks when she points him to the store phone. She comps him a Coke from the machine and slides him the rest of her cigs over the next hour and a half, while he stares at the humming freezer full of mealworms next to the register. Stacey doesn't ask questions. Stacey works the overnight shift at the gas station next to mountain campgrounds known to only diehards. Stacey knows better than to ask questions.

In the end, they send three cars: a state trooper, a tow truck, and a park ranger. They ask him questions in triplicate and fuss at the blood on his clothes before bundling him into the back of the ranger's car to retrace his steps. In the back of his thoughts Russ is glad he left the bolt gun on the road, or thinks he remembers doing that. The officer is squinty enough as it is.

Condensation drips over his fingers as he clutches the 32oz to his chest. He lets the trooper berate him for blocking both lanes. You have to pull to the side, son. You could cause another wreck. You could lose your license. You could lose your job. Don't you know better? Russ stares past him into the trees, until the ranger comes into his field of view:

"You said it was a deer?"

Three pairs of headlights ogle the gaping wound of his windshield, still smeared with gore. It's hard to watch. Instead, Russ watches the headlights themselves, so out of place here,

PERRY MEESTER

hypnotic and comforting. It makes his eyes water. He can't look away.

"She's sick," he says. "Shouldn't have been able to walk. But she ran off. That way. Didn't seem right."

The ranger—Russ thinks he might know him—squints so deep his eyes disappear into his bushy dark brows. "She walked away from *this*?"

There are chunks of skin and bone on the truck and the road. The bumper sags to the ground split in two. She broke her neck, she broke her neck, and the headlights are *so* bright, starting to burn into his vision.

"She's sick," Russ repeats, and hiccups. It makes him want to giggle, which makes the giggle stick in his throat, which turns into a cough the Coke won't ease. "I got her out of the windshield and she ran off. That way. She didn't get out of the way."

The state trooper turns the flashlight straight to Russ' eyes, and his muscles lock.

"Bud, you feelin' okay tonight?"

"I mean, she saw me. She wasn't *scared*."

"You wanna get your license and registration out of the car for me?"

"You'll need to catch her. She's sick." He presses on, trying to find the ranger past the light glare. "Something bad. I know. I know what they look like when they're sick. Somebody should put her down."

There are questions, papers, discussions. The light burns halos and sparks into his vision that last far after they wrap a foil blanket around his shoulders. He ends up in the back of the trooper's car, after they say something about *doctor*, and he's not sure he answered right about the drinking or the drugs, the way they're whispering. The trooper warped the ride into a demand and not a question. He's blunt and white and husky, fingers hooked into his belt loops while he talks to the mechanic, so Russ is thinking on how they all look the same, cops on Appalachian roads. They're all bald blank-faced hunters he meets at the scenes of wrecks, gun in hand. Half the time they've dispatched the hurt deer before Russ ever arrives.

Russ doesn't register that he's in the back seat until they're on the road. The trooper grunts, shifting in his seat. His eyes flicker to the mirror every so often. The way ahead of them is a tunnel of blinding light, just the yellow lane lines.

She bounds, rather than steps, into the road. Before that very moment she's uncertain, maybe a trick of the light, a blur solidifying into reality in the headlights. Hair mats in dark clumps and sticks to a flash of rib breaking through skin. Her jaw hangs loose, her tongue a pink ribbon. Her teeth grin, grin, grin. Her legs hold her upright despite their shattered angles. Her neck twists her head to the left, so only one eye is visible.

She is devastated, and the teeth that grin are slightly too many, slightly too human. As the cop slams on his brakes and Russ is thrown forward, seatbelt biting into his chest, he thinks he hears her chuckle, guttural and drowning. He thinks he chuckles back.

The second thing he does is vomit sugar water onto the rubber floormat. Somehow one hand frees himself from his seatbelt while the other pushes at the door. Locked, but the doe's impact jostled it free, enough to slam his shoulder again and again until it deposits him on the forest floor. Pine needles and old litter dig into his palms and face.

"Hey." Russ says it three times, since he gags on the first and chokes on the second. "Hey, hey!"

The cop twitches. Blood pools in the lines on his forehead.

She dangles, stuck on the cruiser's grille. One leg is shoved between the thick bars, and her ribcage presses into the metal as effortless as clay. She makes little mewling sounds, one hoof pawing at the ear. When Russ limps to the front of the car she locks eyes with him. A soft wet rope of intestine slips from gouges in her belly, hanging outside like a second misplaced tongue. She doesn't blink. It sticks him to the road.

"Sorry," he says, for no reason other than that he feels he should be, and that he is. "I'm sorry now. I am."

When she starts to laugh it's so terrible that Russ backs away not consciously, but out of deep-borne instinct. His feet want to take him to safety. His eyes want to follow the headlights, not the doe between them. Bile rises in his empty stomach. As he turns to spit it to the side, he's interrupted by a dry-twig crackling.

The doe yanks her leg from the grille. It has become something unrecognizable, but it still finds purchase against the car. Her body heaves entirely,

48   GHOULISH TALES

onetwothree, crunching to free itself, smacking to the asphalt.

Russ runs down the center of the road, at first a backpedal, swiveling to break into a full sprint. The service station is miles away and the mechanic and park ranger will be long gone; his phone is missing, NO SIGNAL and all. None of it would help. He's in the backwoods deep-down Something Else where the tree line will slurp him down whole if he strays too close.

In the end, when his chest burns for lack of oxygen and the tears streaming down his cheeks are tripping him up on the curving parkway, he stops, unable to push further. Looking back reveals—nothing. She's out there, but she moves at her own pace, nothing but a suggestion when he strains into the shadows. All he hears is his own heavy panting.

When Russ stares at the scratches on his hands he's not sure where he got them. Glass from the broken windshield worming beneath the gloves; twigs from the roadside; something he doesn't remember. The moon is bright above him and the stars are sharp. He's waiting. For her, or for something worse. Just not for help.

The doe comes in her own time. She comes with the sound of rasping bone as she hobbles on demolished limbs. Her insides are a slow drip trailing behind her, dislodged with each limped step. She clicks her tongue at him in greeting.

"They take you home and eat you," he tells her. The bitterness in his own words is a surprise. So caustic he could puke. "If you're not fucked up too bad. So it's not even *for* anything."

She shakes her head, back and forth, back and forth, as she joins him to the side of the road. He needs, he understands, to cradle her—to hold her upright when her body fails her. He needs to bash her skull in with the nearest rock. He needs to step on the gas until the engine bursts into flames. In her eyes is hate, hate, hate.

It's not always deer that die at the side of the road. Sometimes the ambulance comes too late. Metal bends in weird ways, or a seatbelt isn't clipped; the cars with flashing hazards have blood on the airbags and inside the windows, and hell, half the time Russ gets to listen to the crying.

His hand is big enough to wrap around her skull. Even with the shaking he knows there's strength in it. She leans into the touch—around the adrenaline he still feels the teeth clamp into his arm. Light and testing, dissolving into pinpricks of hurt as she gnaws lightly, just enough to break the skin. Worrying down into muscle, tearing strips.

A motor slices through the forest hum. Tons of steel propelling forward on roads the cops don't watch too close, working down the mountain. Russ' head whips back to catch the first gleam of headlights flickering through the trees, bouncing off the shadows of foliage and creatures, catching orbs of watching eyes.

The doe's pupils contract against the light. She has green eyes, beautiful eyes, shoved misshapen into sockets that don't fit them just right. She tilts her head at Russ, freeing his arm, smiling with pieces of skin stuck between her teeth. He has to lean close to hear the whisper on her fetid breath.

"Figure it out yourself."

Goddamn, but aren't those headlights bright.

In their efforts to avoid the creature that leaps into the center of the lane, the single driver loses their wits. They yank on the wheel, their mouth opening and forming into silent curses, tires squealing frantic on the road, too late to brake sharp. Russ doesn't have the time to tell them that when you encounter an animal on the road you should never swerve—you should hit it head-on, duck your head, trust the brakes and the car to keep you safest. Instead of folding him into the grille or launching him over the top or sucking him beneath the wheels, the car clips his side, bringing the ground crashing up to meet him. The world splits into a deafening roar. A horn blares and then cuts off.

The doe has lost her ability to laugh, so her roadside exaltation is more like a scream.

Curled fetal, Russ cannot scream the way he'd like. There is blood sprayed across the windshield of a car wrapped around a tree. There is the bite of loose debris biting into his cheek where it molds to asphalt. There is hot rust in his mouth. There is the pain radiating out from a thousand individual points, mostly in his leg, where he feels the cold of bone pushed through skin and so can't bring himself to look.

Joke of all jokes, there's no comfort, and no explanation.

She runs a warm, bloodied tongue through his

hair, pasting it down to his forehead, savoring his shudders. She clicks in the back of her crushed throat. Her blood paints the parkway a mile back the way his puddles. She loves his body annihilated; she's giddy, content, affectionate. All forgiven. When Public Works scrapes them both off the road neither of them will be dinner material. They'll puzzle over the scene for months.

"Just lay down," he coughs. "Just right here. C'mon." Dawn is coming in hazy violet and dawn is always coldest.

The doe huffs. It takes her agonizing minutes to drag her failing corpse a yard away, but when she collapses her eyes stay on his, burning triumphant. The deer on the side of the road usually die alone. Sometimes with a bullet in their brain, sometimes like this, bleeding out before Russ can arrive. Their families in the trees, if they stay to watch, don't dare keep them much company once they've jumped.

He jumped—right at that car. The headlights are burned onto his retinas and blurring with the rest of it. He jumped, unsure why, but she dared him, and he jumped. Should make him angrier. Should be hurting more than the slow pulses of ache that fade out with every breath.

The doe dies first. Her body is fragile, and so, so tired. She leaves him to the trickle of anger that turns into a laugh. On a good night, it can take an hour for the sirens to make their way up the mountain. Plenty of time to keep wondering why.

THE WINDOW AT MY MOTHER'S BACK, THE DOOR IN MY BELLY

A. W. Prihandita

BEFORE THE FIRST WORD I uttered, before my lips even bloomed, before my brain was anything more than a collection of cells the size of a fingernail, I remember dangling from the hole at my mother's back, sweeping left and right, left and right, my umbilical cord a flesh-and-blood swing. Mother would sing me a nursery rhyme, and when fingers sprouted from the stumps that became my palms, I learned to grasp her hair and hold on, swaying to her tempo as she danced a circle around her grave. We had the best home: right under a kemboja tree and by a huddle of jasmine shrubs, so fragrant I never knew the smell of blood or rotting flesh.

Mother said her grave released her because she promised to raise a good girl. She was dead, then she breathed anew, her unaborted shame becoming new flesh, new hope: me.

She carried me for nine months, like any good woman would. When I was too big to nest inside her, she let me crawl upon the velvety ground of the graveyard. She taught me to cross myself and give thanks for the heartbeats in my chest—give thanks to God and the grave pit that released us. We made a pilgrimage to the gravestones of the men who killed her. Which of these gravestones was my father, we didn't know. Mother said it didn't matter; what mattered was that we got a second chance, and they didn't.

She was the one who put them in their graves.

Murder paid with murder, terror with terror. She used to walk the streets at night in her long white robe, hunting down the men who hunted her, to all eyes a beautiful woman right up to the second she spilled their guts.

She wouldn't do that anymore since I was born. "From now on, we are good girls," she said. "We are a good, respectable family. We are humans."

But the truth was, we weren't really humans. She was a ghost, a living dead. I was half a ghost only by virtue of the promise Mother made to her grave pit. I'd be more human—in spirit if not in physique—if I grew up to be a good girl.

When Mother said we were good and respectable, this was only a vow, not yet a statement of truth.

***

"This is how you become human," Mother said on the day we were to leave the graveyard. She was gone for a few hours and returned with a shopping bag, which she hid behind her back like thieves would hide the things they stole. "I'll pay for everything later," she mumbled.

She cast off her white robe, baring her ashen skin and the bloody hole at her back. I stared at it—the window of my fetal months—and glimpsed back into her, at her spine and the coils of her intestines. Maggots feasted in the hole as if her flesh never ran out.

All that disappeared behind the white shirt she pulled from the shopping bag, layered with a stiff black blazer that concealed her hollow. A black pencil skirt completed the look, and when she turned around, I almost didn't recognize her.

"This is how you become human," she repeated. She sprayed perfume all over herself, though it barely concealed her jasmine-and-funeral balm smell. Next came a bottle of foundation, smeared all over her skin until she was the color of a ripe sawo fruit, not death. A lipstick came last, blood red but not bloody. "Look alive," she whispered.

Then she wiped smudges of dirt off my face and helped me with my new dress. I understood dressing up was to be a ritual, and I was never again to crawl on the graveyard ground, or play hide and seek with headstones, or learn to read by spelling the names of my mother's rapists and murderers. Those were things that the child of a sundelbolong would do, but I? I was to be human. I was to be a good girl, a second chance made good, a promise fulfilled.

She took my hand, and together we walked toward a new life.

***

For the first day of school, Mother packed three stabs of satay with rice, some leftover karedok, and a slice of papaya. No milk, because we weren't perfect, and Mother already worked too hard to wrest the satay from the street hawker. "There has to be some meat," she declared, and no matter how we were doing, it must never be her own meat. She carefully portioned her meager shopkeeper's salary for proper meat.

She taught me many kinds of smiles and ways to introduce myself ("But never tell anyone what your mother is, remember that.") I dreaded handshakes, fretted over the coldness of my ghostchild skin, but Mother said at least I was warmer than her. If anyone ever asked why I felt cold, I should blame the air conditioning, or just bat my eyelashes and blush, like their presence was so radiant it made me nervous.

"To be human is to have friends," Mother said.

I did all she suggested. I tried to be kind and make friends. When I learned origami, I folded cranes for every kid in the class, each in their own favorite colors. I must've folded a thousand cranes throughout elementary school, but none of them flew. Most ended in the trash bin, a colorful flock of failed friendships. I never understood what I did wrong; truly, all I ever did was be a good girl.

Nothing made me feel more misplaced than the end of each semester, when our parents must come to pick up our report cards. Most of my classmates

would come with both of their parents, and there I was, wringing my cold hands and dreading the moment my teacher would shake my mother's colder hands—or worse, when someone would ask where my father was.

I always said my father was dead, which was not a lie, but not the whole truth either. They didn't question me—until the end of the first grade of junior high, when Mother came to pick up my report card. We waited outside the classroom with the other parents and students, and when my teacher finally called my name, Mother stood and walked toward the classroom door.

My classmate Raka crashed into her back in the middle of his sprint down the corridor.

Shock stilled his face as he peeled himself off Mother's back. Mother turned ashen, more death-like than usual. A deeper black bloomed on her stiff blazer, the taut fabric that covered her hole. I knew if Raka were to crash into her again, there would be a smudge of red against the white of his uniform shirt.

When the summer break was over, I returned to school amidst a storm of whispers and snickers directed my way.

"Her mother's back is hollow," Raka said, forever the unruly child.

"Her mother is a sundelbolong," the rest of them said. "A ghost, a monster."

"No wonder her father's never around. She must've killed him."

"Hey, ghostchild! Do you walk okay? Are you floating?"

"You feel cold. Gosh, it's true, isn't it?"

"Sundel—"

"—a prostitute—"

"—bolong!"

"—with a hole on her back!"

"Your mother is a whore!" Raka jeered.

I snapped. Of course I knew what sundelbolong meant, but when he said "whore," he didn't say "used to." He wasn't talking about the past; he was saying she was a whore *now*. He didn't know—wouldn't care even if he knew—about the insult he threw at the vow my mother made to give me life. *From now on, we **are** good girls. We **are** a good, respectable family. We **are** humans.*

I screamed and lunged at him. My fingers like claws, my legs floating off the ground like I was the ghost he wanted me to be. I landed upon him wielding nails as my weapon, drawing blood from his cheek, leaving a long trail of torn skin down his cursed leg.

"My mother is a shopkeeper!" I shouted. A shopkeeper at the shop from where she stole my first clothes. She was someone trying to pay for sins that weren't even her fault. She wasn't a whore.

Raka's friends jumped into the fray. We were on the floor, a tangle of limbs. Cold floor, warm limbs. Hard floor, vicious limbs. But I was only a pair of arms and a pair of legs, while they were many; I was still trying to be a good girl, while they hated me with the boundlessness of children who were born unconditionally.

Our teacher lectured us about fighting, but did nothing else. I cried, partly for the pain, partly for the guilt and sense of failure blooming in my ribcage. Raka told me to shut up and pinched my arm until it turned red then blue. The bloody scratch on his cheek now sat upon the corner of a sneer, and his eyes glinted with vengeance.

The next day, his father came to school and demanded my expulsion. My teacher arranged a mediation. I begged her not to go, but she went anyway. Our cheeks burned under the jeers my classmates hid behind their palms, but Mother just drew her blazer closer around her and held my hand.

I was suspended, but not expelled. When I returned, everything got worse. *Whore, sundelbolong, bastard girl, ghostchild*—these were my names now, scribbled by my classmates on the blackboard, carved on my desk and chair, shouted across the classroom and the school yard. They stretched out their legs before me and feigned surprise when I tripped—"Why aren't you floating, ghostchild?" I became the color of blue bruises and red-hot shame.

Mother noticed. She said, "Be patient, my good girl."

So I was. And because of that, the bruises never had the chance to disappear. They grew blacker and more numerous, and Mother noticed this too.

One night, I was woken up by the front door clicking softly closed. Mother was no longer in bed next to me in our cramped room. I flipped the light switch on and saw the drawer of her vanity gaping open—the drawer that held her long white robe from her ghostly years.

Ice slithered down my guts. *No, Mother, no. Didn't you promise?*

I ran out and called for her, but she was gone. I ran back to our room, turned the lights off. Hid under the blanket, closed my eyes shut. I counted the seconds and minutes and hours against my trembling breath, praying she wasn't doing what I thought she was doing.

It felt like forever before the front door rattled open again.

No footsteps. Tears rolled down my cheeks, but I kept my eyes shut. The bedroom door opened. Still no footsteps. A whispered swish, the sound of a long robe being shed to the floor.

A weight sank at the foot of the bed. A long silence, and then, a muffled sob.

I couldn't help myself, I cracked one eye open. Mother was sitting at the edge of the bed, facing away from me, the maggots in her back wriggling under the pale moonlight from the window. She cradled her face in her hands, surrendering her sobs to the secrecy of her palms. But I heard those sobs all the same, and I wanted to answer with a scream.

She'd tried so hard. *I don't do that sort of thing anymore,* she'd said when I was born. But here she was anyway.

She picked herself up and shuffled to the bathroom. In her nudity, I saw the blood on her hands. I had to suppress a gag.

She was in the bathroom for hours, her sobs muffled by the shower. When she was done, she sat at her vanity and frantically smeared foundation all over her, as if being the color of a living human would erase her ghostliness—her monstrosity—off her body.

In the morning, our bedsheets were streaked with the brown that had rubbed off her as she tossed and turned in the wee hours of the morning. I pretended not to see. I couldn't stomach another reminder of what my mother was—what I'd forced her to be.

At school, I heard that Raka's father had been murdered in his bed.

***

The cross pendant glittered under the sunlight when Mother held out the necklace for me. "Wear this under your clothes," she said. *As a reminder to be good*, she didn't say.

After the murder, Mother became obsessed with going to church. But we never actually went inside the church building; we'd come late when all the pews had been taken, and sit outside in the overflow area with plastic folding chairs. There was a kemboja tree in the yard, and it reminded me of our old home, the graveyard. Mother prayed ardently, but would sneak out before the pastor came to give the sacrament. Whenever we passed the church's open doors, I'd catch her looking longingly at the confessional booths. I suspected she never entered because she was too ashamed, feeling too dirty to step foot in a holy space.

But it was plain she craved absolution. As she should, I thought. And I should too, because that was what good girls would do. Perhaps if I prayed harder, became purer, no one would hurt me anymore.

After his father's death, Raka never bothered me again, too absorbed in his own shock was he. And because there was another sensational gossip they could obsess over, my classmates left me alone. I spent the last grade of junior high with my chin tucked neatly to my chest, being quiet as a dead mouse, praying they wouldn't notice me or remember anything about my sundelbolong mother.

Graduation meant freedom. For nine years, Mother had worked her bones to death to support my education, but after what happened, I had no interest in returning to that cage and letting people throw more rocks at me.

Over a dinner of a fried rice portion split in two, I told Mother I would leave our small town and find a job in the capital, in Jakarta. She grew wordless and contemplative, chasing shreds of chicken and fried shallots around her plate.

"Yes," she said at last. "I'll come with you."

She said it almost like a question, timidly, like she was asking for my permission. I glimpsed at her face, at the sadness of abandonment painted on it, even as she carved me an encouraging smile. The rice in my mouth turned dry like sand. When I finally swallowed, I swallowed also the glimmer of possibility that maybe, maybe I'd rather go alone.

"Of course, Mother," I said.

We booked a one-way ticket to Jakarta and packed our belongings. We were already a few steps out of the front door, dragging our heavy secondhand suitcases, when Mother staggered, stopped, turned around and went back inside.

She returned with her long white robe. She had left it in her vanity drawer, but now she smiled sadly and said, "To be human is to make peace with yourself. Even if you're still trying to be better."

We found a tiny home in a kampong at the edge of the city, where the houses leaned close against one another, trying to hold their bricks together. The street was barely wide enough for a motorcycle, and always at the threat of flooding from the narrow, clogged gutters. Mother found a job at a nearby restaurant. I was hired as a cashier at a department store in a shopping mall, closer to the city center.

I carefully budgeted my incoming salary. Near the mall, I found a room that I could afford: a cramped one, just enough for a bed and barely anything else. To Mother, I said the commute was too long; I should rent my own place.

"I'll visit you often," I promised. "We're still in the same city, but it'll save me a lot of energy and some transportation money, compared to if I make the trip daily."

I said this gently and with a twinge of guilt, but I held firm. With the same sad smile she gave me when I told her about moving to the capital, Mother nodded her permission. "You've grown," she said wistfully. "You're a good girl. I'm proud of you."

I couldn't help but think her words still sounded like a wish, not yet a statement of truth. But I must admit this, if only with shame: the first night I spent in my new room—my *own* room—and found none of her jasmine-and-funeral balm smell in the air, I felt a little more human.

***

Her name was Anisa, and she worked in the makeup section of the department store. I spent most of my first day at work staring at her from behind the cash register, trying hard not to gawk. She seemed to glitter under the store's fluorescent light.

She noticed me around lunch time, giving me a cheerful wave from across the floor. "New girl—hi!" I frantically rubbed my palms together when she strolled over, and when I took her extended hand, I prayed I was warm enough for her.

She brought me to a warteg in the alley behind the mall, and paid for my modest portion of jackfruit curry over rice. "This will be my first and last time treating you," she said with a laugh, oblivious to how this was my first time being treated by anyone. "I don't have a lot of money to throw around."

She complained about her long commutes in trains so packed she could barely breathe, almost being swallowed by the platform gap multiple times as the crowd carried her mercilessly. Without thinking, I offered to share my new bedroom. Half the rent, help each other out. She took my hand and held my coldness between her warmth. "Really? You'd do that for me?"

I never had a friend before. I remember Mother said this was one of the things that made you human.

Anisa took me mall-hopping. The malls were the different chambers in the city's heart; they thumped with life, and they let you breathe in a light, soaring way, unburdened by the weight of heat, humidity, and pollution of the city's open air. We romped through a dozen department stores. She showed me how she'd visit different makeup counters before her late afternoon shift, trying out new shades of lipstick or mascara brands so she'd arrive at work looking like a polished model, without having to spend a penny.

Dressing up was a ritual. This time, it was a merry one, and we didn't even have to steal like Mother did with our first clothes.

In the room we now shared, I watched Anisa do her prayers, wondering at the soft texture of her prayer mat and the pristine white of her mukena. Her bows and prostrations looked like a dance, her recitations a song. I fiddled with the cross pendant Mother gave me as I memorized Anisa's choreography.

I watched her perform her ablutions too, every time before she prayed. With her lips tracing the shape of a prayer, she cupped her hands under the running tap, pooling water in her palms and splashing it over her face, then rubbed her arms and legs under the little waterfall. The ritual of washing one's body, it looked comforting, I thought—reassuringly carnal.

I wondered if this would be a better way of cleansing my sins than the confessional booths at the church that Mother longed for. I had no sins to confess through the simple abstractness of words. My sins were inscribed in my flesh: the sins of being conceived through impurity, of being born to a sundelbolong.

Anisa had no sins, I was sure. She moved through life with the resourcefulness of a kindhearted pauper, finding ways to survive without resorting to misbehaviors. Five times a day she washed off any impurities she accidentally picked up; there was no time for them to accumulate.

This was what a good girl looked like, I was sure; this was what it meant to be human. Anisa knew it better than I or Mother did. She became my religion; I loved her with all my convictions, and copied every one of her footsteps. In the morning I'd wake up before her so I could hold my finger before her eyes and feel her lashes brush against my skin when she woke.

She died a year after we first met, stabbed with a knife in a robbery, in that alley where we lunched for the first time.

***

What was the point of being human, when the monsters got you anyway?

I wished I'd never tried to believe that the world would be good to you if you were a good girl. Why was Anisa dead, then? She didn't deserve it.

Maybe the sundelbolong that was my mother was right, after all. She was full of sins; she was more monster than human. But at least, here she still existed, while Anisa lay dead in her shroud of purity.

After Anisa's burial, I stumbled to the train station and boarded a train home. The world swam around me, as if I was moving through shifting fog. I vaguely noticed a sense of disappointment when the platform gap didn't swallow me. Bodies pressed against me from all sides, and I welcomed breathlessness.

I had only visited home intermittently since I started my job, and never for more than one night. In the past month, I hadn't visited at all, so caught within Anisa's orbit was I.

The door opened with a long creak, and I realized none of the lights were on even though it was getting dark. I called out for Mother. She answered, faintly, from the bedroom. I found her under the thin blanket, reduced to hollowed bones wrapped in deathly skin.

"What—what happened?" Her knuckles felt as sharp as cliff edges when I held her hand. I wanted to roar in grief and guilt both.

She smiled. "Nothing. Just a cold, I'm sure. Don't you worry. I'm so sorry for your loss. Are you okay?"

I choked out a laugh. "Mother, when have things ever been okay?"

It wasn't just a cold. Mother remained weak for days, then weeks. We didn't dare go to a doctor because of her hollow back, so instead I brought her to a shaman.

He knew immediately that Mother was a sundelbolong. Still, he laid her on a bamboo mat and examined her. It was then, as I stared at her fragile bones through the faint smoke of a burning incense stick, that I realized I never stopped loving her, even in her failure to be human, even as I longed to know a world beyond her ghostly shadow.

"She's losing power," the shaman said. "She's gone too far from her grave, for too long. It's too late to take her back, I'm afraid—she wouldn't survive the journey."

"Don't feel bad," Mother said before I could lose my breath. "I followed you of my own volition. You needed to start living. I was always already dead."

No, Mother, you never died, I wanted to cry out. *Even in your death, you were always very much alive.* But I didn't say it. I held myself tightly coiled, lest I unraveled completely.

"What will become of her?" I asked instead.

She'd grow too weak to maintain her human form, the shaman explained. It took a lot of discipline to be human, and a lot of energy to be disciplined. When she could no longer muster enough energy, she'd become a sundelbolong once more, whether or not she wanted that. She'd roam the streets at night and kill people for their flesh, flesh that would replenish her. She might become human-like again once her energy was restored, but never for long. And so it would repeat.

"Unless you want me to exorcize her," the shaman offered. "A litany of prayers, and she'll disappear."

"No, thank you," I said.

Mother protested. "Just let me go. "You'll be"—her voice broke—"you'll be more human without me, anyway."

I shoved down the guilt from ever thinking that myself. "I want to spend my time with you, for as long as I can," I said firmly.

We went home. I made her as comfortable as possible, all as I watched sanity fade from her eyes. I kept a knife on her nightstand, just in case. I held myself tightly coiled still.

I was there when the light in her eyes finally blinked out. She rose from her bed, her white robe suddenly on her, her feet not touching the ground. She floated toward the door with a bloodthirsty sneer on her face, but I held her with my ghostchild arms.

"Mother, don't you remember your promise?" I exclaimed. "You said you'd be good. We'd be a good, respectable family. Won't you try, try again?"

I unraveled there and then, and with this, all the power I'd been conserving in me spilled out. Once again I had the strength that I had when I fought my classmates, only now it was my own mother I fought, the sundelbolong. She snarled and thrashed against me. I held on, but she finally shook free, though I still clung to one of her hands.

With my free hand, I reached for the knife on her nightstand, and plunged it in my belly. I carved a lump of my flesh and offered it to her.

This must be what children felt like, when they let a stray kitten eat from the palms of their hands. *I love you, little one. Mother, aren't I a good girl?*

Good girls wouldn't feed themselves to others, would they? Such an abomination that would be, inhuman. But I no longer cared if I was a good girl—if *we* were good. Pretending to be human would never save us, not when it didn't save Anisa. All we could do was preserve as much dignity as we could for ourselves, and sometimes, that meant becoming monsters.

Mother was right, that time when she embraced who she was and went to kill the father of my bully.

She ate, and it replenished her. Light returned to her eyes, and before she was fully conscious, I made sure she was back in her bed and cleaned, no trace of my blood on her lips. I found a dark loose-fitting shirt that hid the hollow in my belly. It reminded me of Mother's stiff black blazer.

She fell asleep, and when she woke, she smiled like she never was a sundelbolong. She never regained enough strength to walk around, spending most of her time asleep. Often, she only woke to hunt for flesh. That was my cue to pick up the knife once again and play butcher for myself.

When I fed Mother my own flesh, I became an abomination, but it kept her from becoming one. That was the only grace I could give her. She'd fought so hard for a second life as a human, so I'd give her that for as long as I could. My belly became the only door she had left to humanity.

Sometimes when she gained enough strength, she became lucid and able to converse. In one such moment of sanity, she held my hand and asked, "Have I raised you to be a good girl?"

A lump grew in my throat, and around it I choked out, "Yes, Mother. You made a promise, and you've fulfilled it."

I didn't tell her it was a lie. She didn't realize I'd been feeding her my own flesh; she didn't need to know what I'd become.

"Good, good," she said. Her smile glittered like Anisa's did, and for a second I truly believed we were good.

Maggots started feasting in the hole in my belly as if my flesh would never run out—and I knew it never would, because I was never fully alive in the first place. Never fully human, always half a ghost.

And that is all right. To be human is to make peace with yourself.

To this day, I still feed myself to my mother, shamelessly, like she fed herself to me in my fetal months. When I become so thin and small I have nothing else to give, I will once again crawl into the hole at her back, and curl up into a period. I won't tell her I wish I hadn't been born, but Mother, I so wish to come home.

REVIVAL TOUR

Alex Luceli Jiménez

UP UNTIL RAMONA Perez was killed, Faustina Solano never intended to revive a human. It was a fluke of the universe that she could do something so strange, and it had long since faded into irrelevance by the time she was eighteen. If Ramona had not been killed in a car accident a week after their high school graduation, there may have even come a day when Fau forgot about her power altogether. As it was, Fau knew what she had to do as soon as Ramona's mother called her and broke the news in tears.

Three weeks later, at Ramona's funeral the first week of July, Fau showed up in a little black dress. She did not know if her power would work on a human; she had only ever brought roadkill back to life. She arrived before everyone else, ahead of even her own family. She asked Ramona's parents for time alone with the open casket, closed the black doors leading into the viewing room at the mortuary, approached a body that had been put back together following traumatic injuries, put her hands on either side of Ramona's powdered brown face, closed her eyes, and willed Ramona back to life.

When she opened her eyes again, Ramona was still dead.

For three weeks Fau had kept her grief at bay reminding herself that this moment would come: the moment when she would bring Ramona back to her side. For the first time in her life Fau imagined a life without Ramona. A life without her best friend to argue with and do everything with and sleep beside.

"Come on," Fau whispered. "Come on, Ramona! Come on!"

She shook Ramona by the face. She shook her again and then she pulled her hands away and put them on her own face, her shoulders shaking up and down as a sob built up in her chest, how could this be no no no but it always worked, *it always worked*, Ramona was going to be dead forever *howcouldthatbe* and then—

A heaving gasp, and through her tears, Fau watched Ramona shoot up in the casket, the long brown wig slipping off her sewn-together head.

"The car," Ramona croaked, "the car just drove into opposite traffic and I–"

"Ramona," breathed out Fau, "oh, Ramona."

Ramona's face twisted into horror as she said, "Oh, Fau, you're a goddamn idiot."

"I know. But you'll understand." Fau leaned forward, picked up the wig, fixed it back onto Ramona's head, and smiled fondly as she said, "We have to go."

***

At eighteen, the Roadkill Experiments of 2003-2005 were buried deep in Fau's file cabinet of personal history. Maybe those years should have made a bigger impression, but it wasn't like she could go around bringing animals and, Lord forbid, people back to life just because she knew she could.

There was no art to it. She had a flickering flame in her chest, and she knew she could kindle that energy by focusing on it, and that was all. She did it for the first time when she was in the third grade and she and Ramona found a dead dog on the side of the road while walking to Fau's house after school.

"Don't touch it, Fau," Ramona said, but the flame in Fau's chest was burning bright and something drew her closer to that dead dog. She had never seen a dead thing before. When her fingers made contact with the yellow labrador's bloody corpse, the flame burned brighter than it had ever burned. Without realizing what she was doing, she focused her flame, and watched as the dog started breathing again. Her fingers slipped away as the dog righted itself. It still looked injured, but she watched with fascination as the open wounds in the dog's body started closing up. It was still bloody, and as time would tell, that blood would never quite go away. Then the dog trotted away.

"I think," Fau told Ramona, who had come up next to her, "that I just brought that dog back to life."

It was that declaration that brought on the Roadkill Experiments. Ramona believed Fau about the flickering flame in her chest, and anyway, she, too, had seen the dog come back to life. It took them almost two years to gather five test subjects: three squirrels, a cat, and a mouse. Each time Fau touched the lifeless corpses, they sprung back to life. Each time, she experienced a burst of energy followed by a period of exhaustion and delirious thirst.

Despite all of these test subjects, the dog remained the most damning one. It became a local legend around their inland southern California suburb: the bloody dog that attacks and eats other dogs. It evaded capture by animal control for two years before it was shot and killed in the middle of a dog attack by one of Fau's neighbors. This was towards the end of fifth grade, at which point Fau and Ramona first voiced what they now knew to be true: Fau's power came at a price, so she had to stop using it. More importantly, she should *never* use it on a person. Neither of them subscribed to the Catholic masses their parents made them attend, but they still knew some things were better left to God.

***

Fau drove for an hour before the post-revival exhaustion grew too heavy. On the car floor behind her was an empty gallon jug of water. Next to her

in the passenger seat, Ramona was asleep. By the time they had made it out through the back door in the viewing room that led out to the parking lot, Fau was practically dragging Ramona, who was alive again but nearly dead on her feet. The exhaustion meant that Ramona had gone along with Fau, questioning nothing, not even the suitcases in the backseat of Fau's car and Fau's half-assed answer of *you'll see!* when Ramona asked where they were going and what everyone was going to say when they found out she was alive again.

If Fau had it her way, no one else would ever know that Ramona was alive again. No one they knew would ever see either of them again.

She picked a random exit on Highway 1 and found a motel with vacancies. When she opened the passenger side door to wake Ramona, she had to shake her hard, like she had shaken her in the casket. Ramona started awake and started mumbling gibberish, hands pushing against Fau like she was trying to defend herself. Fau stilled her with a grasp on her shoulders, and said, "I got us a room. Let's get some rest."

They left the suitcases in the car. Fau figured they could get them in the morning so they could change quickly before getting back on the highway and heading north. She had to pull Ramona to their ground floor room, every step of Ramona's dragging, but eventually they got there, collapsing together on the made bed, both of them still in their funeral clothes, Ramona in her ghastly funeral makeup, cherry red lips and golden eyeshadow applied with a heavier hand than Ramona would have done on her own.

Fau would have nodded off the second her head hit the coarse pillow if it were not for Ramona whispering, "Fau, where are we going? How are we getting there? You have to tell me."

"We're driving north on Highway 1," said Fau, and then, because she had never been good at keeping anything a surprise, went on. "We're going to San Francisco to get married like we always said we would, because while you were dead, gay marriage was legalized in California."

"Was it really? You're not messing with me?"

"Would I mess with you like that?"

"No, I guess not. My head's all muddled. It's fuzzy. I can't explain it. I'm so tired."

"Let's get some sleep. You know how I get after reviving."

Fau closed her eyes, and heard Ramona whisper, "Wow."

***

More pertinent in Fau's file cabinet of personal history than the Roadkill Experiments of 2003-2005 was the road trip Fau's parents took her and Ramona on when they were in the sixth grade. They took Highway 1 north to San Francisco, stopping in San Luis Obispo, Monterey, and Santa Cruz on the way. It was San Francisco that made Fau and Ramona's eyes blow open wide, eager to drink up every sight they could get their irises on. They had never fallen in love with a place until that moment. They had never thought of what their future could be until then. It was on that trip in 2006 that Fau and Ramona's life plan was made: they were going to get married and grow old together in San Francisco.

Fau's parents, to their credit, played along, though it wasn't until their third day in San Francisco, as they ate clam chowder at a seaside restaurant, that Fau's dad broke it to them: same-sex marriage was not legal. Two girls, in 2006, could not get married in California. This did not, however, mean that they could not live together. They could even be "domestic partners" if that was what they wanted. It was almost as good as marriage.

"But we want to be each other's wife," said Fau, biting at her plastic straw. Ramona had picked up the habit from her, and was doing the same.

"You can't," said Fau's dad, "at least not yet. Who knows? Maybe someday."

"*But we want to be each other's wife,*" said Fau, again, louder this time, and Ramona nodded rapidly in agreement, and Fau's mom let out a deep sigh.

"Don't say that so loudly, Faustina," said Fau's mom. "Want what you want, but be careful of who you let know."

Fau did not understand it then. Not at age eleven. Not at age twelve, either, or age thirteen. It was not until she turned fourteen that a switch of realization flipped on in her brain and she woke up one day knowing: she wanted to kiss her best friend, but her mom had already told her long ago. Be careful of who you let know.

***

Fau found the articles by Googling her name on her phone with the morning light seeping into the motel room, Ramona still asleep by her side. She was being written about by her local suburb's paper, but also the *Los Angeles Times* and other major outlets which had picked up what was of course a ridiculous story: *18-year-old girl steals body of her dead best friend and runs away.*

She retrieved their suitcases and shook Ramona awake. Ramona's eyes were half-lidded as Fau tenderly cleaned the ghastly funerary makeup off Ramona's once-dead face with a makeup wipe. The wig that so closely resembled what Ramona's hair had looked like in life was slightly lopsided, but had mostly stayed on during the night. Ramona had always been the kind to lie still in her sleep, whereas Fau tossed and turned. Often they woke up with Fau's limbs spread atop Ramona's body.

"Is there life after death?" Fau asked Ramona as she rubbed away at the golden eyeshadow and brown foundation.

Ramona was quiet until Fau got to her red lips with the wipe, and when she started speaking, Fau pulled away to let her talk.

"I don't know how to explain it," Ramona said. Her words were a little slurred, like she had had something to drink. "Maybe time doesn't work the same after you're dead, because all I remember after that car crashed into mine is that you were with me. My head was in your lap and you were singing to me. How could you have been with me?"

"I'm always with you," Fau said, and it came out in a whisper. Then louder: "What was I singing to you?"

"That song you wrote a few years ago. 'You're a dream thing, you're everything.'"

Ramona spoke the lyrics matter-of-factly instead of singing them, and Fau smiled and sang, "'You're my angel wings, you're everything.'"

"'You make my heart sing,'" Ramona said in a half-singing voice, "'you're everything.'"

"'Everything to me,'" Fau said, finishing the verse, singing voice growing quieter, "'everything to me.'"

The silence hung heavy between them for several seconds until Ramona asked, "We're not going to tell anyone else I'm alive again, are we?"

"No, we're not."

"You should have never brought me back. You know what happened to the dog."

"That's not going to happen to you."

"Fau, it's already happening."

Fau said nothing. She finished cleaning Ramona's face, and then they got dressed in a hurry and left. She did not have to tell Ramona why they had to hurry.

It was not until Fau pulled back onto the PCH that she asked Ramona, "How long do you think you can stay in control?"

"I don't know, Fau. I just know I don't feel right."

"You have to be okay," said Fau. "You have to be okay for just a little while more. We're going to go to San Francisco, and we're going to get married."

She braced herself for Ramona's signature retaliation but all Ramona said was, "Okay."

Creeping down the highway at barely the speed limit, Fau felt sick.

**

They were five when they met. They were seated at the same table in their kindergarten class and they were drawing. Their teacher Ms. Castro had asked everyone in their class to draw a self-portrait for the first day of school. Fau wanted to draw herself with pink hair, because she dreamed of having pink hair, but the girl sitting across from her was using the only pink crayon. Instead of getting up and hunting down another pink crayon, Fau told the girl, "Give me that crayon."

"No," said the girl.

"Give it to me *please.*"

"No."

"But I said please."

"I'm using it."

"But I need it, too."

"No."

"Please."

"No."

"Please."

"Shut the fuck up," the girl said plainly, at the very moment that Ms. Castro walked by.

"Ramona!" Ms. Castro was aghast. "That is not appropriate language to use at school, or anywhere."

Ramona did not look at Ms. Castro. She looked at Fau squarely, and looking back, Fau knew her eyes must have been blown wide, her mouth hanging open. Then Fau let out a little huff of a laugh, followed by a shaking full-body laugh. She was laughing so hard and so loudly it hurt, and suddenly Ramona joined in, and both of them were dying of laughter and Ms. Castro was scolding them and to this day Fau cannot remember a single word that Ms. Castro said. Only their breathless, shaking laughter, and what followed when they both had to stay inside during recess.

"My name is Faustina," she told Ramona.

"I'm Ramona. I can't say that. I'm gonna call you Fau."

They both liked the color pink and listening to the Beatles because their dads listened to the Beatles and long drives and Disney movies and playing instruments. Fau loved to sing, had a beautiful low voice even in her littlest youth, and her parents paid for her to learn the piano starting in the first grade. Ramona could barely carry a tune, but her dad played guitar and taught her informally when he had time. She was a natural from the get-go and soon enough, she was teaching herself.

When they were in the seventh grade, they got more serious about music. Fau started writing songs, and Ramona started putting chords to her lyrics. Ramona got a video camera for Christmas at age thirteen and they started filming themselves singing and playing covers of popular pop songs overheard on the radio. They called themselves FR because they couldn't think of anything better. Most of the views on their cover videos came from family members. They were each other's only real friend. Fau was perpetually introverted and Ramona hated everyone except Fau.

So when Fau was fourteen and realized she was in love with Ramona, she wrote a song and called it "Everything." Usually she gave her lyrics to Ramona and Ramona composed them on guitar, but this time, she composed it herself on the grand piano her parents had invested in for their only daughter when they saw how seriously she took music. One Saturday she invited Ramona over and played the song for her. When she was done, Ramona said, "That was intense."

Then she asked what they were going to have for lunch, and Fau knew, in that moment, one thing for sure: she could never tell Ramona how she felt. Even if it meant marrying the love of her life platonically.

***

Next stop: San Luis Obispo. Fau was still feeling the effects of having revived Ramona and it occurred to her, as her eyelids drooped precariously with her hands gripping the wheel, that she had not had anything to eat since yesterday, the morning before Ramona's funeral. They stopped at a diner, Fau wearing a Dodgers cap and not meeting anyone's eyes for too long. She ordered a plate of pancakes and a hamburger and fries and a diet Coke. Ramona said she was not hungry, but Fau made her eat a bite of a pancake anyway. Ramona barely swallowed before she jumped up from the diner booth. Fau was too dumbfounded by the sudden show of energy in an otherwise sluggish Ramona to respond immediately, but after a few seconds she ran after Ramona. When she walked into the bathroom, one of the stalls was open and Ramona was crouched down on her knees, gagging over the dirty toilet and dry heaving. As Fau came closer, she could see that the toilet bowl was full of black liquid.

"I can't," Ramona said in between deep breaths, leaning her forehead down on the edge of the toilet. "I can't eat regular food. You knew that."

Fau thought about what Ramona was like usually (lively, biting, calculated) and what she was like now (subdued, diluted, sickly), and she made a plan.

They went to a grocery store after Fau hastily finished what she could stomach of her diner meal, Ramona's black liquid vomit still lingering in her mind's eye. Fau kept her chin pointed low and led Ramona to the meat section.

"Pick something," she told Ramona.

Ramona picked a packet of pork loin. This was all they bought. As part of her grand plan to revive Ramona and run away, Fau had taken out her college savings in cash: $20,000. A little dwindled now that she had paid for gas and a night in a motel, but it would do. Back in the car, Ramona tore into the package, lifted the meat with her bare hands, and bit into it. Fau watched her chew carefully, then more fervently. Ramona took another bite, and then another. Little rivers of watered-down pink blood ran down her chin. She

closed her eyes in reverence, and Fau let out a breath.

But then Ramona opened her eyes and whispered, "I don't think this is enough."

"I can go buy more—"

"That's not what I mean."

"Just hold on," Fau said, voice strained thin, "just hold on a little while longer."

***

They spent the night in San Luis Obispo and made it to Monterey the next day. If it were up to just Fau's determination they would already be in San Francisco, but reviving a human drained her in a way that reviving animals never did and she was still feeling like no amount of sleep would ever be enough. On the drive they sang along to *Abbey Road* and David Bowie's *"Heroes"* and Elton John's *Honky Château,* Ramona looking a little more alive now that she had her fill of raw meat, and it was almost like it was before Ramona died. When Fau almost hit a car changing lanes, Ramona let out a stream of profanity and scolded her.

"You're such a goddamn space cadet," Ramona said, voice curved into a low shout. "What's gonna happen if you get into a fucking car accident? Your parents don't know where you are, and if we get into a car accident, they will. You think your parents can handle seeing me like this? You think *my* parents can handle seeing me like this?"

"You're right," Fau said, "I'll be more careful."

But by the time they checked into a seaside motel in Monterey, Ramona was sluggish and slurring again. Fau watched her sway side to side in front of the motel window that night from her spot on the queen bed, watched her peel back the curtain a little to peek outside.

"Fau," Ramona whispered, "there's a man out there smoking a cigarette and there's no one else around."

"Okay?"

"Do you think there are security cameras here?"

"Why?"

"Because I'm just thinking that I could go out there and...you know."

Fau straightened up, stood, and to joined Ramona. She pulled the curtain out of Ramona's weak grasp and let it drop so that the outside world was closed off to them. She gripped Ramona by the shoulders and said, "You can't."

"I'm so hungry," Ramona said. Her words seeped into each other. "I'm sososo hungry."

"You just have to wait," Fau said. "Just wait until we get to San Francisco and get married."

"Why? You can't marry me if you know I've killed someone?"

"That's not what I mean. It's just that it's too risky the closer we are to home. After we get married in San Francisco we'll go far, far away and you can eat whatever you want. I promise."

"You're a goddamn idiot," Ramona said, words paired with a shaky breath. "You should have never brought me back. You knew I would come back like this."

"You would have done the same for me."

"I know I goddamn would have."

Fau pulled Ramona down so that their foreheads were flush, and together, they breathed.

***

Fau decided they could skip Santa Cruz and drive straight to San Francisco the next morning. The exhaustion was starting to pass; she was confident she could make the two-hour drive with the help of coffee. She wasn't worried about it. What she was worried about was the way Ramona woke up skittish, eyes bloodshot, body jerking at every sudden sound and movement. In her first life she was adamant about never slouching, and now she was hunched over, holding her torso like she was trying to keep herself together. Fau piled her into the car and told herself they could deal with it later.

As she made to shut the passenger door, Ramona reached out in a flighty movement and gripped Fau's wrist tightly.

"What?" Fau asked, trying to shake her hand away. That only made Ramona grip tighter. Finally her grip went lax, and she let go.

"Nothing," Ramona said. So they went.

Back on Highway 1, Fau realized almost too late that her car needed gas. She pulled over to a little gas station in an industrial area where there was nothing else and no one around except a gas station attendant wiping down the windows of the attached food mart. As she fixed the nozzle into the tank, she leaned against her sedan, closed her eyes, and sighed deeply.

When she next opened her eyes, Ramona was standing in front of her, bloodshot eyes narrowed, and then Ramona's hands were on her throat.

"I'm sorry, Fau," Ramona slurred, "but I'm so hungry."

"Ramona," Fau whispered, or tried to whisper, but the air was already being squeezed out of her, and she watched Ramona bare inhumanly sharp teeth, *how had she not noticed those teeth*, and then—

"Get off her!"

Ramona had to let go of Fau's throat when the gas station attendant pushed her. Fau did not have time to stop what happened next. Her wild gaze caught the gas station attendant, a scrawny teenage boy with a large name tag reading *Ignacio* hanging from his red polo shirt. She was paralyzed as Ramona lunged at Ignacio, knocking him down to the concrete ground easily; she was taller than him, had more meat on her bones.

Fau only started to hear herself scream when Ramona ripped out the boy's throat with her teeth, blood splattering every which way, drops of it landing on the toes of Fau's white low top canvas sneakers. Ramona snarled as she ripped away the red polo t-shirt and started biting into what meat there was in the boy's midsection. The sounds she made as she ate were moans of innocent pleasure, like a child delighting in an awe-inspiring sight. There was relief in those moans, too, and the screams died in Fau's throat as Ramona slowed down her feasting and looked over her shoulder to face Fau.

Now Ignacio was nothing but a mangled face, bones that were once part of a torso, and splayed legs in bloody blue jeans. Ramona's legs were crouched on either side of his hips, her spine curved over his remains as she chewed. The ends of her brown wig were wet with blood. Her hands were bright red and her green t-shirt was so soaked that parts of it looked black. Worst of all was her face, her teeth still bared and her cheeks and forehead smothered with the red liquid that had once kept Ignacio alive.

"I was hungry, Fau," Ramona said. "Don't look at me like that."

That spite sobered Fau up. She straightened, and looked around. She came forward, and held out a hand to Ramona to help her up.

"We have to go," Fau said. "We have to go now."

Like some unseen force was controlling her, Fau started the car and pulled back onto the highway. She drove in silence for a long stretch of road. Her knuckles were white on the steering wheel.

When her face started to tingle, that strange thing that sometimes happened to her when she was having a panic attack, she clenched the steering wheel tighter and took the next exit on the highway. It led her to a dirt backroad outlined with thickets of cypress trees. She pulled over to the side of the road. She left the car on, opened her door, stepped out, and screamed.

She screamed for a long time. In the distance she could see a gate leading up to a blue house and maybe whoever lived there could hear her but no one came out, and then Ramona was in front of her like she had appeared in front of her at the gas station, and Ramona's bloody hands were on her cheeks and Fau's cheeks were probably bloody now and Fau was still screaming and Ramona was saying, "Get a grip."

Ramona said it again: "Get a grip. Get a fucking grip, Fau."

Her throat hurt too much to keep screaming. She swallowed hard and tried to jerk out of Ramona's hold, but Ramona was holding on too tight. Even with her eyes open and focused on Ramona's face, her beautiful face, all she could see was Ignacio's gnawed corpse.

She wondered what would have happened if she had revived Ignacio. She wondered if his consumed flesh would have grown back.

She opened her mouth to scream again and what came out was, "It's just that I love you, Ramona."

"I fucking know that. Don't you think I fucking know that? You goddamn revived me and you knew you weren't supposed to. You knew what would happen."

"You don't get it. I love you."

"I told you I know."

"No, Ramona. I love you like I'm in love with you. I love you like I don't just want to get married to you because you're my best friend." The cotton was less now. "I thought I couldn't tell you but then you died and all I could think about was that I never told you and I should have."

"I know, Fau."

"No you don't—"

"Yes I do. You think I don't love you too?"

"Not like that—"

"You think I want to marry you as a joke?"

Fau was almost holding her breath when she said, "You want to marry me because we're best friends."

"It's always been more than that." Something was blazing in Ramona's eyes. "You have to know it's always been more than that. You think I'm not too much of an idiot to tell anyone how I feel? Of course I love you too. But saying it is harder than anything else in the world."

"You're saying it now."

"I had to die to be able to say it."

At that, Fau let out a breathy laugh, followed by an actual laugh. Ramona chuckled, too, and then Fau was reaching out and pulling Ramona against her, blood and all. She wrapped her arms around Ramona's shoulders like she had so many times before, feeling Ramona's chest against hers.

When she pulled back, Ramona leaned in with that flighty, jerky way of hers and kissed Fau. It was an open-mouthed and wet kiss. It tasted metallic and Ramona's sharp teeth caught on Fau's bottom lip and it hurt.

"It's okay," Ramona told her as she pulled away. "I know what you have to do, and it's okay. Death isn't so bad."

"I'm sorry."

"Don't be sorry. We had a good time."

"You were telling the truth?" As Fau asked this, she lifted her hands to grip Ramona's throat. "About me singing to you after you died?"

"You know I was."

Fau tightened her grasp on Ramona's throat.

"Then I'll see you there."

DO YOU BELIEVE IN MISTER BONES?

I BELIEVE IN MISTER BONES

Max Booth III

ENJOY THIS EXCERPT OF
I BELIEVE IN MISTER BONES
BY MAX BOOTH III.

I believe in Mister Bones, and by the end of this book so will you.

THAT'S HOW THE manuscript started, although Daniel didn't know that yet. He thought he was still reading a cover letter. Only nutcases copy/pasted an entire book's text into the body of an email. Anybody who knew shit about shit used attachments. Word docs, usually—watermarked PDFs, if they were paranoid.

DO YOU BELIEVE IN MISTER BONES? the subject line had read.

It'd caught his eye as he scrolled his phone on the toilet. He assumed it was spam at first. Someone trying to sell him dick pills. Most people, Daniel included, deleted those types of emails without bothering to open them. But there was something about this one—*who is Mister Bones?*—that wedged a lemon of curiosity into his brain.

Plus, he'd initially misread the name as *Mister Boner*, which was undeniably hilarious.

He read the first line, then registered how much text proceeded it, and started scrolling, and scrolling, surrendering long before reaching the end. This was a fucking book submission. A long one. No title listed, either. Not even a byline. The sender's email address was equally cryptic: augustskeef@yahoo.com. Augustskeef? What the hell kind of word was that? First and last name, maybe? August Skeef? Augusts Keef? Either option sounded equally ridiculous.

He tried reading a few more sentences of the manuscript, but his train of thought derailed at the sound of someone else barging through the door. For a moment, he'd blissfully forgotten he was sitting in a shopping mall restroom. The sudden explosion of moist flatulence from the stall next to him shattered any delusion he might've constructed for himself while scrolling through his emails.

With one swipe of his thumb, he deleted the bizarre email, then finished his business and flushed. There were five sinks in the bathroom, and only one of them ever seemed to work. Which one that was, however, changed weekly—almost as if by design. They were all motion sensored, so Daniel stood in front of each basin waving his hand back and forth for a couple seconds. The last sink he approached ended up being the one that'd decided to be operational this weekend. It was always the last one he tried. Anything to make him look like a fucking idiot.

Cold water blasted from the faucet with the intensity of an industrial sand blaster, hitting the porcelain and splashing all over his stomach. There was no way these sinks were up to code. He doubted anything in this mall would meet any standard regulations. The front of his shirt was soaked. Considering how hot it was in this building, he didn't mind getting a little wet. But still. He'd need to dry off. Nobody wanted to buy books from a guy with wet hands. He went over to the towel dispenser and waved at the sensor. Nothing happened. He slapped it a couple times. He whispered a few desperate pleas. Nothing came out. It was empty. Of course it was. He wiped his hands on the back of his shirt and got out of there before the neighboring stall's occupant could confront him about causing a commotion. The man would soon find himself in the same predicament, and only then would he understand what Daniel had gone through.

By the time he exited the bathroom, he'd already forgotten about the unsolicited submission.

Their vendor table was in the middle of the mall, on the ground floor. If they'd gotten stuck upstairs again, they probably would have bailed before setting up. The mall only had one elevator. It was typically cramped and shook as it lifted and declined, like it might collapse under any amount of extra weight. Everybody always joked about how this place was haunted. Despite working in the horror genre, he didn't really believe in that kind of shit, but for this mall he could almost make an exception. The story went, sometime back in the early 1960s, while installing one of the elevators, an unlucky contractor got himself stuck between the elevator doors and then, as these things sometimes went, was fully decapitated. Now, supposedly, the poor fucker's headless spirit haunted the property. It was a good story. He kept meaning to turn it into a zine or something to sell exclusively at these little popup events. People around here would've eaten it up.

There were also two sets of escalators, but neither had been operational in all the time they'd been participating in events here. So, at least two years now, and they were still broken. Daniel'd once asked one of the ladies who operated the coffee shop in the food court how long they'd been

out of order, and she gave him a look like she didn't understand the question, as if it was silly to assume there'd ever been a point in time when they *had* been functioning. The discolored caution tape blocking off the escalators didn't show much promise that maintenance planned on addressing the issue any time soon, either.

Reaching the table was a bit of a challenge. The mall was packed. Sweaty nerds cosplaying as their favorite slashers and oblivious, argumentative families doing their absolute best to block every conceivable pathway. Maneuvering around them was its own type of stupid sport. Weekdays, this place was dead, but on weekends when there was an event going on? Every goddamn person in San Antonio seemed to make an appearance.

The event organizer, Xiomara, knew their shit when it came to promotion. They hosted something at least once a month, sometimes twice, depending on how close in the year it was to Halloween. This was the second consecutive year Daniel and his wife Eileen had purchased the $1,000 vendor package, which reserved them table space at every Ghouls & Boils-organized event for the next twelve months. Xiomara first launched G&B as an annual festival every October—then, as it grew in popularity, expanded it into a full-time business. Eileen and Xiomara had gone to high school together. From the way Eileen once explained it to Daniel, they hadn't exactly been best friends or anything, but they'd been friendly enough to keep in touch post-graduation. Their shared interest in horror movies kept their paths slightly aligned, Eileen full-on embracing the horror lit community and establishing Fiendish Books with Daniel while Xiomara took a stronger interest in spooky merch like shirts and Funko pops, ultimately leading to the creation of Ghouls & Boils—now a bi-weekly multi-themed popup market featuring over fifty vendors at the American Utopia shopping mall *plus* a permanent brick and mortar located within the same building.

It was easy to spot Daniel and Eileen's table. For one thing, they were the only book vendor. Everybody else sold stuff like plastic DIY Halloween jewelry, low-quality bootleg art prints, used DVDs inexplicably marked at retail prices, and those tall Jesus candles with famous slashers like Leatherface and Ronald Reagan stickered over the holy savior. But also, their banner stand towered over the masses of sweaty mall customers like a lighthouse beacon guiding him to safety. On the left of the banner was their logo, a rotting zombie head deepthroated by a butcher's knife, courtesy of the cartoonist Betty Rocksteady, a weirdo Canadian who handled the majority of their artwork needs:

And to the right, in red goopy font, was the name of their press:

FIENDISH BOOKS

There was only one person browsing their selection, an older fella dressed primarily in blue denim, from his jeans to his buttoned-up jacket. Eileen remained seated behind the table, working on her laptop—most likely formatting the interior of an upcoming Fiendish publication—and that told Daniel everything he needed to know about the potential customer: he was a nutjob. Normally she would have been standing and greeting whoever approached their table and asking questions to help ensure the sale—unless the person turned out to be crazy, then she'd avoid eye contact and hope like hell they didn't try engaging in any further conversation. Daniel considered waiting until the guy left before officially returning to the table, but noticed Eileen had already spotted him and was motioning for him to hurry.

The moment he slipped behind the table, she said, "Gotta pee," and fled the scene before he could ask any follow-up questions.

He glanced at the denim guy and nodded. "How's it going?" he said, too many years of previous customer service jobs kicking in on instinct.

Unfortunately, the guy took this as an invitation to start a dialogue. He leaned over the stacks of horror books at their table and said, in a voice that sounded like steamrolled gravel, "You a publisher?"

Daniel gulped and weighed his options, then gave him another nod. "Yup."

"You publish scary books?"

"We, uh, try to." Daniel had to take a step back from him. He reeked of hard liquor and unwashed ass.

"Let me tell you something," the man said, "I've just spent the last fifteen years of my life living in Central Mexico. I have seen some shit. Some *real* shit. You know what I'm saying?"

"Uh, no, not really."

"I'm saying I've witnessed some shit that is *really* scary. The shit in movies? That doesn't scare me. But this shit? It's real-life shit. It's actually scary."

"Oh, okay," Daniel said, scratching the back of his neck, "that's cool, man."

"So what do you think? You want to publish it or what?"

"Publish . . . ? Did you write a book, or . . . ?"

The denim drunk shook his head. "No, I'm telling you, this is *real* shit. But it could be a book. It'd be scarier than any other goddamn book out there, I fuckin' guarantee it."

Daniel despised getting caught in these types of situations, which always seemed to happen whenever they were vendoring somewhere. It almost felt like they were holding him hostage with the slim chance of them possibly buying something at the end of their interaction. That was never the case, of course. These types of people were never interested in actually supporting the arts. The sad, pathetic truth was they had nobody else to talk to anymore. Their friends and loved ones had stopped responding to their messages. They had run the well dry and were now desperate for any kind of human connection. Somehow that then became Daniel's responsibility. "Well, we aren't exactly open for submissions right now," he explained, "and even if we were . . . we'd only consider finished manuscripts—not, uh, pitches."

"What do you *mean*, exactly?" the guy asked. "You want me to, like, take something to a printer and get it bound?"

"What?" Daniel tried not to laugh, immediately failed. "No, I mean . . . a digital file. Microsoft Word or Google Docs or whatever you have available. You'd email it as an attachment."

"But there's no book."

Daniel shrugged. "I guess you'll have to write it."

"Hmm." The drunk studied a stack of Fiendish titles on the table between them. "Tell you what," he said, glancing back up at Daniel, "what if I just, like, compile everything into a list, and send that your way?"

"A list?"

"Yeah, a list of all the fucked-up shit I've seen."

"Like what?"

The drunk hesitated, as if afraid someone else might be eavesdropping, and whispered, "You don't even want to know, man."

"But I thought you *did* want me to know?"

"Would a list work, or not?"

Daniel shook his head, wondering if Eileen had already finished peeing and was somewhere nearby waiting for this guy to leave, just as he'd tried to do before she caught him in the act. "We don't take a look at lists. You'd have to write it as a book."

"But don't you think something like that would sell, though?"

"I don't know. It's hard to say. Even a book containing the craziest, scariest material isn't going to mean anything if the writing's bad."

"The writing?" Something in the drunk seemed to deflate.

"At the end of the day, yeah," Daniel said, "the writing is what matters most. It's what guides someone through the story. If the writing sucks, then nobody's going to read it."

"What if I've never written a book before, though?"

"Then, I don't know, I'd suggest practicing a lot. What kinds of books do you typically read?"

The drunk stared at him like he was being asked an impossible question. "I only read one book, sir."

Daniel was sure he'd misheard him. "You only read one book?"

But he'd heard correctly. The drunk nodded. "The Holy Bible."

Daniel waited for the drunk to start laughing. It didn't happen. "You only read the Bible?"

"Yes, sir. It's the only book that matters, far as I'm concerned."

"Then . . . why do you want to write one?"

The drunk shrugged. "I just don't know what else to do with all of these experiences I've had."

Daniel sighed. Goddammit, where was Eileen? Now *he* had to pee again. "Well," he said, biting his lip until the pain made him stop, "I guess I would have to strongly discourage you from trying to write a book, then, if you have no interest in reading books besides . . . uh, the one you mentioned."

"What do you mean?"

"I mean, man, it's pretty insulting to come here and tell me—a publisher—that you don't read books, all while trying to get me to publish something of yours, which you haven't even written. You don't get that?"

"Hmm." He glanced down at the books again, then nodded. "Okay, sir. Thank you for your time." He turned around and stumbled over to the next vendor table. The man's smell, sadly, decided to linger awhile.

Seconds later, Eileen slid up next to Daniel and said, "What a fucking nutjob."

She happened to say this just as three children approached the table, ages ranging anywhere from seven to ten, if Daniel had to guess. Although it was hard to tell for certain, considering all three were cosplaying as horror monsters: Freddy Krueger, the Babadook, and the Creeper from *Jeepers Creepers*.

"My mom says you're not supposed to say 'nutjob,'" Freddy Krueger said.

"Yeah," the Creeper added, "it's apple cyst."

"*Ableist*," the Babadook corrected.

"Oh."

"It's true," Daniel said, shaking his head sadly. "I'm always telling her that."

"I'm very sorry," Eileen said, holding back a laugh. "You're right."

"What does your shirt mean?" the Babadook asked, pointing at Daniel's chest.

He glanced down, having already forgotten that he was wearing his favorite T-shirt of all time, one that he frequently wore in public despite Eileen's protests.

Against black fabric, in large white letters, the shirt read: I CAME ON EILEEN.

"Oh," Daniel said, and nodded at his wife standing beside him, "it's, uhh, from a song."

Freddy Krueger picked up a book from their table—*Misfortunes* by Mindy Rose—and started flipping through it. "What's this book about?" he shouted. Then: "These drawings are very gross."

Misfortunes was one of the few *experimental* titles Fiendish had published. Its appearance closely resembled a children's book, which definitely seemed to attract the attention of children at popup events—something Daniel weirdly never anticipated, perhaps because he was an idiot. Every page was illustrated in color by Betty Rocksteady. As Freddy Krueger commented on, the art *was* gross. But it was also incredibly hilarious. The illustrations were accompanied by brief, one-to-two sentence "death predictions" written by Mindy Rose, some weirdo they'd connected with on Tumblr several years ago.

Examples of misfortunes found in the book consisted of entries like *You will die the exact same way as Amelia Earhart (suicide by cop)*; *Congratulations! You've just been cast in John Landis's segment of* Twilight Zone: The Movie; and *You will discover a snake in the toilet. The two of you will fall deeply in love and live together for 12 years, until one of you is diagnosed with a terminal illness and you decide to each swallow cyanide capsules while listening to your favorite album in bed.*

Not *exactly* for kids—but, not *not* for kids, either, as far as Daniel was concerned. The shit was funny no matter how old you were.

"It's a book that predicts how you're going to die," Daniel explained.

All three of the kids seemed flabbergasted by this concept.

"*What*?" Freddy Krueger said, and slammed the book back down on the table. "Why would you want to know *that*? You can't avoid death no matter what. Why would you want to *know*?"

The Babadook shook his head and yelled, "I avoid death all the time! It's easy!"

"Even if you *try* to avoid it, it's still going to get you somehow." Freddy Krueger said. "Like . . . like . . . like what if it says you're going to die 'in bed' and then you stop using a bed . . . what if a bed then *falls on you from an airplane?*"

"Whoa," Daniel said. "I never thought about it like that."

"I would step out of the way," the Babadook replied.

"No you wouldn't! You wouldn't even see it coming until it was too late! You would be killed just like everybody else!"

"I want to die from AIDS," the Creeper said, matter-of-factly.

"Uh, what?" Daniel said, suddenly uncomfortable with this interaction. Where the hell were their parents, anyway?

"*Old* AIDS," the Creeper clarified.

"Old *age*?" Eileen asked, and the kid nodded inside his mask.

"You know," Daniel said to the Creeper, "that costume you have on? The person who made that movie is a convicted child molester."

"Huh?" the Creeper said.

Eileen nudged him with her elbow. "*Daniel.*"

"Victor Salva. That's his name, the guy who made *Jeepers Creepers*. Look it up sometime," Daniel said. "Seriously, it's pretty messed up. I'm sure he still profits from the franchise, too, and yet they continue releasing new ones every couple years."

"What on earth are you talking about, mister?" the Babadook asked.

"What's a child molester?" Freddy Krueger asked.

"How do *you* not know that?" Daniel asked. "You're literally dressed as one."

"I am?" he said, surprised.

Next to him, the Babadook started laughing at his brother and shouting, "You're a child molester! You're a child molester!"

"Molester! Molester!" echoed the Creeper, as all three of them seemed to lose interest in the book table and scampered off to the next vendor.

"What the hell is wrong with you?" Eileen asked, once they were gone. "Are you trying to get us arrested?"

"What do you mean? Of all people, shouldn't *children* be aware of the concept of child molesters? Like . . . they're the ones who need to watch out for that stuff! If anything, I'm doing a public service here."

"I'm sure your medal is in the mail."

"Also, wait," Daniel said, "come to think about it, for kids raised by someone who's already educating them about ableism, isn't it *extra* nuts that their mom wouldn't also be aware of someone as problematic as the *Jeepers Creepers* pervert? Where does this woman draw the line, right?"

Eileen stared at him for approximately ten seconds before saying, "I'm so glad we never had kids."

The rest of the day didn't see many sales. A few bites on their discounted back-issues of *Fiendish*

Tales, mostly because they were cheap and the cover art caught the eye. That was fine with Daniel, though. The writers in the magazine had already been paid their one-time flat payment pre-publication, which meant there were no royalties to keep organized. Any magazine sales went straight back into the company—or, in situations like tonight, would pay for their dinner.

Loading out always felt a hundred times more miserable than loading in. When a vendor was setting up for an event, there was a certain whiff of optimism in the air. *Maybe all of this shit will sell,* they might think, *maybe the universe will provide a sign I am not wasting my life producing art nobody cares about.* This almost never happened, of course. Even on weekends with heavy foot traffic and customers with money to burn, there was always an embarrassing amount of stock left to box back up come Sunday evening. Maybe the solution was to bring less stock, but there was always that fear of running out, of not having that one perfect book for that one perfect reader. So they tended to overprepare, and they paid the price afterward.

While Eileen returned stacks of books to the empty boxes under their table, Daniel went out to their car to fetch the dolly. Nearly a decade ago, when they first launched the company and started vendoring at popups and conventions, the concept of requiring one of these things had never entered their minds. They'd instead lugged each box from their car to the venue, then back again once the event wrapped. It was a tiring, time-consuming process that they'd quickly grown to dread, but the idea to head over to Home Depot and buy an actual dolly didn't form until after vendoring at the city's first Alamo City Comic Con. The convention itself—that initial year, at least—proved to be more successful than anticipated, but it was the load-out experience that ended up forever traumatizing them. Once ACCC shut its doors to the public, vendors were told they had exactly one hour to pack their shit and get out before the warehouse's garage exits were locked, which was already an insane expectation, but now consider the fact that due to either poor organization or miscommunication or perhaps a little of both, this load-out period also happened to coincide with the San Antonio Zombie Walk—meaning streets were shut down, and none of the vendors could retrieve their vehicles from the parking lot several blocks away from the Henry B. Gonzalez Convention Center. Most of the vendors had dollies, and thus faced minimal trouble transporting their stock to the parking lot. Daniel and Eileen, on the other hand, were shit out of luck and forced to carry stacks of boxes around hordes of citizens in zombie cosplay who all insisted on being in character, which meant none of them understood what the words "excuse me" meant and instead tried to get in the way as much as possible. Some of these dorks were even lunging at people and pretending to take bites out of them. It was a nightmare. They each had to make this trip at least half a dozen times. Books are heavy, after all. And zombies, Daniel and Eileen concluded, suck ass. So after that, yeah, they finally went and bought a dolly for the company. They would never do another event without one—in fact, if the dolly wasn't actively in use, it would remain in Eileen's trunk, as the fear of forgetting it one day greatly outweighed the annoyance of always driving around with a large metal object sliding around in her car. And they certainly would never do another event during a goddamn Zombie Walk. After that night, the two of them could barely stomach zombie *movies.*

Outside the shopping mall, people were pissed. Some bozo had parked their van in front of the sidewalk ramp, preventing anyone else from rolling their dollies down it. The bozo in question was another vendor, someone far too oblivious of their surroundings to realize they'd need to share this space with others. Half a dozen different vendors lined up in front of the van with their own dollies, growing furiously more impatient by the second. Daniel considered hanging around to see what happened once the owner of the van returned to the scene of the crime, but at the same time he was starving and sick of being at this fucking mall, so he maneuvered around everybody and headed over to their SUV in the center of the parking lot. He popped the trunk and dragged out the dolly, then wheeled it back toward the mall just in time to overhear the blocked vendors giving shit to the van owner.

"Wow," one of them said, "I sure wish there was a communal ramp for us all to use right now."

"You know what I love?" another said. "Standing on sidewalks doing absolutely nothing while my children wait for me to pick them up from the babysitter."

Daniel wheeled his dolly past them all and stole an amused glimpse of the bozo nervously loading several boxes of trademarked horror movie shirts into his van. He was drenched in sweat and something told Daniel it wasn't entirely from the exercise.

Back inside the mall, Eileen had already finished refilling the boxes with books and was nearly done folding up their tablecloths. "There you are," she said. "Another five minutes and I was afraid I'd have to call in a rescue team for you."

"You should see what's going on out there," Daniel said, and explained the situation as they layered the book boxes atop the dolly.

"Wow," she said, "some people have no clue, do they?"

"How'd y'all do this weekend?" someone asked behind them, causing both Daniel and Eileen to flinch. Xiomara—the main organizer of these shopping mall events. Shorter than Eileen, but also muscular in a way that secretly intimidated *and* aroused him. He was pretty sure they could knock him out with one punch, if it came down to it.

Eileen recomposed herself first. "Oh, I guess we did okay."

"Yeah?" Xiomara frowned, seeing through the lie. "I don't think we sold much, either. It's weird. Sometimes we can get this place packed with people, but that doesn't always translate to sales."

"If only we could force them to spend money," Daniel said. "Like, by gunpoint."

Nobody laughed at his joke and Daniel scratched his head, thinking, *What if I killed myself right now?*

"It can be tricky," Xiomara said, scratching their shaved scalp, "attracting the right balance of people interested in both the celebrity guests and our vendors. A lot of times, they only come to get something signed by one of those *Walking Dead* idiots or whatever, which I know is a disappointment to everybody else, but sometimes it also translates into extra sales, depending on the person and what, you know, the vendors have available." They paused long enough for it to feel weird. "Anyway, that's why we try to notify our vendors of each event's theme months beforehand, so y'all have time to prepare."

This month's theme was *The Lost Boys,* because Xiomara had dished out the cash to fly Corey Fieldman to San Antonio for the weekend. Unfortunately, Fiendish had yet to publish anything about vampires. Although, even if they had, Daniel doubted it would have made that significant of an impact. That wasn't how book readers worked. They approached tables because they liked to read, not because they were searching exclusively for stories that reminded them of a specific movie from the 1980s. Or maybe that's exactly how readers behaved. If he knew the secret formula, he probably wouldn't be wasting his time every month at this haunted shopping mall asking strangers, "What do you like to read?" and grimacing at one of two standard responses: *Oh, a little bit of everything*—which, of course, was a lie—or, *I wish I had the time*—which was one of the more infuriating responses to hear, because Daniel was sure they had plenty of time to binge twelve seasons of some insufferable sitcom they'd already watched a dozen times before.

"Anyway," Xiomara said, "I'm sure this is all stuff y'all are gonna be finding out first-hand soon. Isn't your festival coming up?"

"Kind of," Eileen said. "We still have another couple months."

"Plenty of time," Daniel said, although he had no idea what he meant by it. Plenty of time for *what*, exactly?

"Well, you know," Xiomara said, "if you guys ever need any help, or anything, I've had plenty of experience, as you know, and I'd be happy to lend a hand."

As they said *lend a hand*, they looked directly at Daniel and smirked in a way that made him uncomfortable and slightly hard. He readjusted his stance, hoping nothing was visible against jeans.

"Um," he said, clearing his throat.

It wasn't the first time in recent years he suspected they might've been flirting with him. Not that Daniel was someone who others went after, often. There'd only been a few occasions, from his recollection. He'd once gone on a podcast where it'd quickly gotten out of hand, in a way that left him thinking, *Wait a second, did I just get sexually harassed?* Another time, at a bar, a woman had leaned into his ear and whispered, *You smell so good,* and left it at that. He hadn't minded that interaction so much. In fact, he'd ridden high off of it for weeks, months. To this day, he still applied the same coconut body lotion after every shower. And when it came to Xiomara, things became more complicated. The flirting wasn't *unwanted*. He would be lying to himself if he claimed he hadn't instantly found himself attracted to them on day one of Eileen introducing the two of them early on within their relationship. Not that Daniel was a cheater, or anything. He'd never betray Eileen like that. Besides, suppose the opportunity presented itself, and he *wanted to*, he wasn't built to be that type of person. He was way too fucking anxious to balance adultery. The stress would eat him alive. The confidence to please multiple lovers sounded like an alien skillset he'd never come close to touching. Once, while masturbating in the bathroom, he'd attempted to fantasize about all three of them being intimate together, but the logistics of a threesome—*even in his own imagination*—were so nerve-racking that he couldn't finish himself off, and gave up.

"Thank you," Eileen said. "That's really nice of you. We don't really know what we're doing yet, but I'll hit you up when we do."

"If y'all ever wanted to come over for dinner, or whatever, to help plan stuff, I'd be open to that, too," Xiomara said.

Holy shit, Daniel thought, *this is exactly how threesomes happen.*

"Well," he said, "we better get going," and quickly pushed the dolly away before anyone else could respond.

It would be another ten minutes before Eileen found an escape from the conversation and joined him outside. Only then did he remember they'd left their tables back in the mall, and he had to run inside to collect them. Fortunately, Xiomara was no longer anywhere in sight.

ABOUT OUR GHOULS

Joe Koch writes literary horror and surrealist trash. Their books include THE WINGSPAN OF SEVERED HANDS, CONVULSIVE, INVAGINIES, and THE COUVADE, which received a Shirley Jackson Award nomination in 2019. His short fiction appears in numerous publications such as Vastarien, Southwest Review, PseudoPod, Children of the New Flesh, and The Book of Queer Saints. Joe also co-edited the art horror anthology STORIES OF THE EYE. He/They. Find Joe online at horrorsong.blog and on Twitter @horrorsong.

Xochilt Avila (they/them) is a queer, non-binary, and multiracial author who currently resides in Maryland, USA. These experiences, living outside of binary labels, have helped foster their appreciation for the uncomfortable, the uneasily defined, and the unloved. Outside of horror, they love playing video games and tabletop RPGs, getting lost in the woods, and fulfilling the whims of their cats. Follow them on Instagram @xochiltavilawrites and Bluesky @xavilawrites

Amanda Cecelia Lang is a horror author and aspiring monster-slayer from Colorado. As a diehard scary movie nerd, her favorite things are meta-slashers, '80s nostalgia, and the rise of a fierce final girl. Her scary stories haunt the dark corners of many popular podcasts, magazines, and anthologies, including *The Deadlands, Gamut, Cast of Wonders*, and Flame Tree's *Darkness Beckons*. Her short story collection *Saturday Fright at the Movies: 13 Tales from the Multiplex* (Dark Matter INK) is now available. You can stalk her work at amandacecelialang.com—just don't be surprised if she leaps out at you from the shadows.

Lor Gislason is a writer and occasional editor from Vancouver Island, Canada. Ask them about their current hyperfixation or their cat Pierogi Platter and they'll love you forever.

Temple, who writes as **T.T. Madden** (they/them) is a genderfluid, mixed-race writer with stories most recently in the *Dead Letters, Embodied Exegesis*, and *Skin* anthologies. *The Familialists*, their debut social horror novella, is available now, their mecha/kaiju novella *The Cosmic Color* later this year, in addition to forthcoming books with Mad Axe Media and Timber Ghost Press. They want to write books in as many genres as possible, twisted through the lense of scifi, fantasy, and horror. They can be found on whatever social media still exists as @ttmaddenwrites.

Perry Meester spends more time writing than he should, and the rest of the time watching movies that make him feel bad. He loves good coffee, bad music, tragic stories, and every other strange little freak on this earth. You can find him most places online @meatpunkperry. His debut novella, *The Flesh Inherent,* is out now through Ghoulish Books.

Violet (she/her) is a trans writer and MFA candidate at St. Mary's College of California. Her first short story appeared in *Bury Your Gays: An Anthology of Tragic Queer Horror*.

Anselma Widha Prihandita (she/her) is an Indonesian speculative fiction writer, college writing instructor and PhD candidate in rhetoric and composition, with scholarly (and personal) interests in decolonial and transnational writing. She splits her time between the US West Coast, where she currently teaches and studies, and Indonesia, where she grew up and where her home remains. She attended the Odyssey workshop in 2023 on their Fresh Voices Scholarship, and the Clarion workshop in 2024 on their Octavia Butler Scholarship. Her stories are published or forthcoming in *Clarkesworld, Cast of Wonders,* and *khōréō* magazine, among others. You can find her on Bluesky, Twitter, and Instagram with the handle awprihandita.

Alex Luceli Jiménez is a queer Mexican writer and school counselor based in Santa Clara County. Her stories have appeared in *Berkeley Fiction Review, Barren Magazine, Southwest Review, Moonflowers and Nightshade: A Sapphic Horror Anthology, Scissor Sisters: An Anthology of Sapphic Villains,* and others. Currently, she is revising a queer young adult horror novel as part of the WriteHive Mentorship Program. She was born and raised in southern California. You may learn more about her work at alexlucelijimenez.com.

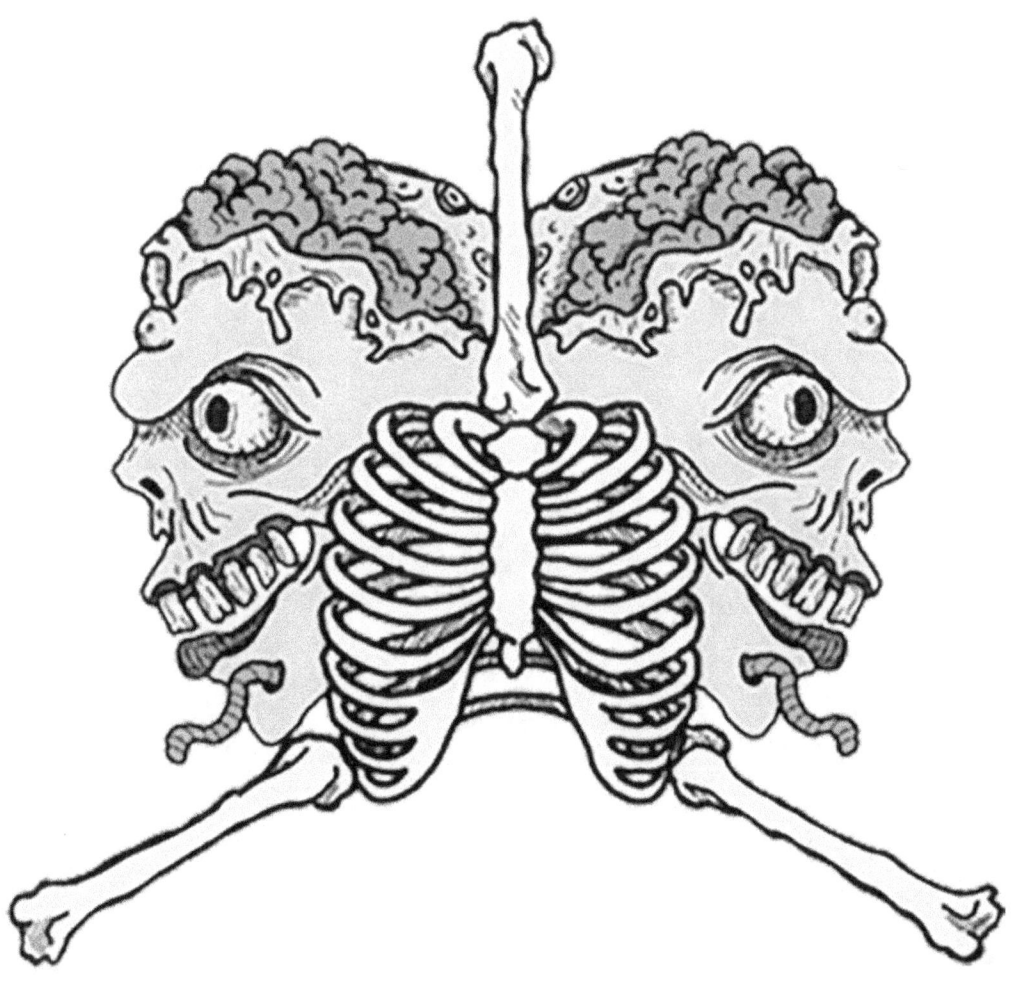

www.ingramcontent.com/pod-product-compliance
Lightning Source LLC
Chambersburg PA
CBHW080841250626

47161CB00009B/3150